CW00819767

DRE

The flowers were beautiful—two dozen dainty white daisies with bright yellow centers, tied with a huge pink bow. A small envelope dangling from the bow caught Marylou's eye. Her fingers trembled as she carefully plucked the envelope from the bouquet, opened it, and pulled out the card. "To Marylou . . . with all my love." She read the words once, twice, three times, unable to believe what she was seeing.

Marylou's heart began to pound as she hugged the flowers to her chest, careful not to crush a single petal. "This isn't a joke," she whispered excitedly. "This isn't a dream. This is *wonderful!*" The whole thing seemed too good to be true. She'd been sitting around depressed all night, and the whole time somebody somewhere loved her!

Somebody out there loved her . . . but who?

Bantam titles in the Sweet Dreams series. Ask your bookseller for any of the following titles you have missed:

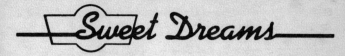

DREAM DATE

Carla Bracale

BANTAM BOOKS
NEW YORK · TORONTO · LONDON · SYDNEY · AUCKLAND

RL 6, IL age 12 and up

DREAM DATE
A Bantam Book/April 1991
Reprinted 1991
Reprinted 1995

Sweet Dreams and its associated logo are registered trademarks of Bantam Books, a division of Bantam Doubleday Dell Publishing Group, Inc. Registered in US Patent and Trademark Office and elsewhere.

Cover photo by Pat Hill

All rights reserved.
Copyright © 1989 by Cloverdale Press, Inc.
No part of this book may be reproduced or transmitted in any form or by any means, electronic or mechanical, including photocopying, recording, or by any information storage and retrieval system, without permission in writing from the publisher.
For information address: Bantam Books.
This book is sold subject to the Standard Conditions of Sale of Net Books and may not be re-sold in the UK below the net price fixed by the publishers for the book.

ISBN 0-553-28295-6

Published simultaneously in the United States and Canada

Bantam Books are published by Bantam Books, a division of Bantam Doubleday Dell Publishing Group, Inc. Its trademark, consisting of the words "Bantam Books" and the portrayal of a rooster, is Registered in the US Patents and Trademark Office and in other countries. Marca Registrada. Bantam Books, 666 Fifth Avenue, New York, New York 10103.

Printed and bound in Great Britain by
Cox & Wyman Ltd, Reading, Berkshire.

To my friends,
for your love and support.

Chapter One

The giant ant crawled slowly out of the huge anthill and onto the brown dirt of the desert. Its large mouth gnashed and clicked in warning as its beady black eyes darted around in their sockets. The clicking noise increased as the insect's eyes focused on an abandoned Army jeep. The ant approached the jeep, moving clumsily on its huge legs. Then, in one rapid motion, the giant ant grabbed the jeep up in its powerful jaws, eating it as if it were nothing more than a cupcake!

Marylou Watkins stared at the television, totally uninterested in the vintage 1945 horror movie her parents were watching. The only horrifying thing about the evening in Marylou's opinion was the fact that it was eleven-thirty on a Saturday night and she was home with her parents instead of out on a date. That was definitely horrifying!

This has to be the most boring night of my life, Marylou thought, twirling a strand of her shoulder-length, dark-brown hair around a finger absently. She turned her attention back to the television, where the giant ant was now chasing a woman who was screaming as she ran. *How incredibly stupid! How could this possibly pass as entertainment?* She shifted positions and expelled a long, deep sigh.

"It's a shame Lori had to go visit her grandparents this weekend," Marylou's mom said, smiling sympathetically. "Usually if you girls don't have dates, you get together and do something fun. I'm sure spending a Saturday night with your parents isn't exactly at the top of your list of great things to do."

"Let's just say it's right up there with having the measles and going to the dentist." Marylou grinned, then stood up and stretched her arms overhead. "I guess I'll just go to bed."

"What? You mean you don't want to see

the end of this riveting film?" Her dad smiled teasingly.

"Dad, the only thing scary about this movie is that somebody actually spent money to film it," Marylou said, laughing.

"Actually, I think you're right." Mr. Watkins stifled a yawn with the back of his hand. "I think I'll go to bed, too."

"What? And miss the end of this great classic?" Mrs. Watkins teased her husband.

"I agree with Marylou," Mr. Watkins said. "I can safely say that I can spend the rest of my life without knowing if the killer ant eats all the inhabitants of Los Angeles! Besides, I should be in the store early tomorrow morning."

"Oh, no, not on Sunday," Mrs. Watkins protested, rising from the sofa and turning off the television. Marylou's dad owned his own hardware store, a thriving business that demanded a lot of his time. "You spend so much time at the store, one of these days you're going to come home looking just like one of those lawn mowers you sell!"

"Goodnight Mom, 'night Dad," Marylou called out to her parents as she walked down the hallway to her bedroom. She giggled to herself as she thought about sitting down to dinner with her mother and a high-powered lawn mower.

"Goodnight, honey," her mother and father answered before going to their own room.

Once in her room, Marylou changed out of her jeans and sweatshirt and into her nightgown, then ducked into the bathroom. After brushing her teeth and washing her face, she smoothed on some moisturizer, critically surveying her reflection in the bathroom mirror. For the most part, Marylou liked the way she looked, or at least she knew how to make the most of what she had.

She had blunt-cut straight brown hair with wispy bangs and big brown eyes. Her nose was straight and her mouth was nicely shaped. People often told her that her best feature was her deep dimples. Her only real complaint was that her cheekbones weren't prominent. But for the most part, she thought she looked okay. Still, she couldn't help wishing that there was something more exotic or unusual about her looks, something that would really make a guy sit up and take notice. She sighed as she thought about yet another dateless weekend. Then she turned out the light, carefully made her way across the darkened hall to her room, and crawled into bed.

She lay there for a moment, listening to the noises of her parents getting ready for bed. Within minutes, the house fell silent except for the occasional familiar hum of the radiators.

I wonder what Lori is doing right now, she mused, thinking of her best friend, Lori Mason. On impulse, Marylou sat up in bed, switched on her bedside lamp, and picked up the telephone. She quickly punched in Lori's number, listening as the the Masons' answering machine gave its message. After the beep sounded, Marylou spoke.

"Lori Mason, I can't believe you went off and left me all alone this weekend. I've never been so bored in my life!" She paused for a moment and grinned. "And if you ever go off and leave me alone for a weekend again, I'm going to call Harold Longview and tell him how you stole his English paper in seventh grade, hoping he'd call you to help him make up the assignment!" Marylou giggled as she thought about Harold Longview. Both Marylou and Lori had been crazy about the dark-haired boy. Marylou had tried to capture Harold's attention by blatantly flirting with him. She had walked with him to class and had called him for assignments that she pretended to have missed. Lori had been more subtle in her approach. She had found out Harold's favorite colors, then wore outfits in those colors each day. In addition to stealing his English paper, she'd found out he liked country music, then had hummed country tunes whenever she was near him. Fortunately, Harold hadn't liked either one of them, so their friendship hadn't suffered any major casualties. "You know I wouldn't really call him," Marylou added. "I just wanted to tell you how lonely it's been here without you around, especially on a Saturday night! Oh, well, I better hang up now, before I use up all the tape on this machine. I'll talk to you when you get back. Call me as soon as you get in!"

Marylou hung up the phone, turned off the light, and snuggled into her pillow. She and her best friend Lori were about as different as two girls could be. Marylou sometimes envied Lori's organized intellect. Lori never made a decision without thinking through all the options. Marylou believed in jumping into any situation with both feet, then thinking about her options after the fact. If Lori didn't stop going about things so methodically, she was never going to *live*!

Still, together the girls were a great combination, and had a lot of fun. *If Lori were home we could have gone to the Pizza Pub where all the kids hang out on Saturday nights*, Marylou thought.

"If only I had a date tonight," she sighed aloud. Marylou's dating philosophy, until a month ago, had been to date whoever asked her out. "Variety is the spice of life," she always told Lori, who was much more selective about whom she dated. In fact, for the past two months, Lori had been steadily dating Walt Sawyer, the president of the computer club. Walt spent most of his spare time at the computer center, but at least Lori had the security of knowing she had a boyfriend!

Marylou hadn't been so lucky. In the past month, she had spent a torturously long date with Tommy Silvers, who had discussed the symptoms of some horrendous skin disease he thought he had. And she had had a date with Jeff Richards, who'd taken her to a car demolition derby. The derby itself hadn't been so bad, but Jeff had spent the rest of their date at the diner rehashing every crash, complete with sound effects. Marylou had wanted to sink through the floor and disappear!

After that incident, Marylou decided that

maybe Lori had the right idea about dating after all. Lately, she had been much more selective, but doing so certainly resulted in fewer dates!

After the boredom of tonight, Marylou was almost willing to believe that a bad date was better than no date at all.

She flipped over on her back and stared up at the dark ceiling. *What I need is a real boyfriend,* she thought, *a serious boyfriend, not just casual dates to pass the time on boring Saturday nights.* Marylou hated to admit it, but it had been particularly difficult since Lori had started going with Walt. She often saw Lori and Walt walking together in the halls at school, holding hands and exchanging furtive kisses between classes. Personally, Marylou thought Walt was sort of a geek. After all, he'd rather program a computer than go to a party, and he'd been voted the boy most likely to become a brain surgeon! Nevertheless, whenever Marylou saw Walt looking at Lori as if she were the greatest thing since the microchip, she couldn't help envying her best friend.

Restless and not a bit sleepy, Marylou got out of bed and walked over to open her window. She rested her elbows on the sill and stared out into the night, allowing the cool, late autumn air to wash over her face.

Marylou's bedroom was located at the front of the house, giving her a full view of the street. The houses along the block were all dark, and there was complete silence except for the rustling of the few dead leaves left on the trees and the barking of a dog. Marylou sighed as she brushed her hair from her face. It should be a sin for an almost-sixteen-year-old girl to be home and bored on a Saturday night!

She turned her head as headlights suddenly illuminated the street, and watched with interest as a car crept slowly toward her house. As the car passed beneath the glare of a streetlamp, she noticed that it was a dark-blue Mustang with a hatchback. *I can't wait till I can drive and own a car like that. But that will definitely be a while,* she thought ruefully. Suddenly, the car pulled to a stop right in front of the Watkinses' house. Marylou frowned, wondering what the car was doing. Her frown deepened as she saw something fly out of the car window and land on the front lawn. Vandals?

"I love you, Marylou!" a male voice yelled, the shout shattering the quiet of the night.

Then with a roar the car sped off down the street and disappeared into the darkness.

For a moment, Marylou simply sat at her window, staring at the place where the car had been only seconds before. She rubbed her eyes, wondering if she was dreaming. "I'm definitely hallucinating," she mumbled to herself. "I've been so bored, I'm actually dreaming up a secret admirer who yells romantic things from his car window!" But despite her words, a shiver of excitement danced up and down her arms, giving her goosebumps.

"There is only one way to find out whether or not I'm losing my mind," she said, jumping up from the window and fumbling in the darkness for her robe and slippers. She yanked her fuzzy slippers onto her feet, then threw her robe around her shoulders, unable to keep the grin off her face. Very quietly she crept from her room, down the hallway to the front door. She carefully unlocked the front door and eased it open slowly so as not to wake her parents.

"This is probably a big joke," she whispered to herself, trying not to get her hopes up. "I'll walk out there and find a bag of trash in the yard. Somebody from school probably threw his garbage in my yard and yelled that he loves me as some kind of weird dare."

Marylou looked first to the right, then to the left, not wanting any neighbors to see her wandering around the front lawn in the middle of the night. They'd think she was crazy! As soon as she saw that the coast was clear, she ran quickly across the lawn until she spotted something reflecting the glow of the moonlight. In the pitch-black night, she couldn't tell exactly what it was. *It's probably just some junk*, she thought disgustedly. *Some people's humor is really gross.* She reached the spot where the stuff lay and her breath suddenly caught in her throat as she looked down and saw exactly what was lying in the grass. *A bouquet of flowers!* Thrilled, she grabbed the flowers and ran all the way to her room. Then she pulled down the shades at her window and flipped on the bedroom light.

The flowers were beautiful—two dozen dainty white daisies with bright yellow centers, tied with a huge pink bow. A small envelope dangling from the bow caught Marylou's eye. Her fingers trembled as she carefully plucked the envelope from the bouquet, opened it and pulled out the card. "To Marylou . . . with all

11

my love." She read the words once, twice, three times, unable to believe what she was seeing. No one except her parents had ever said those words to her!

Marylou's heart began to pound as she hugged the flowers to her chest, careful not to crush a single petal. "This isn't a joke," she whispered excitedly. "This isn't a dream. This is *wonderful!*" The whole thing seemed too good to be true. She'd been sitting around depressed all night, and the whole time somebody somewhere loved her! She frowned as a sudden thought struck her. There was no way to know who her secret admirer was! Somebody out there loved her . . . but who?

Chapter Two

"Start at the beginning and tell me everything again," Lori requested, bringing her car to a halt at the stop sign and turning to look at Marylou. She had picked Marylou up for school a few minutes earlier, and Marylou had immediately plunged into the story of her mysterious midnight visitor.

Marylou sighed, trying to hide her impatience. Sometimes Lori's skepticism drove her crazy. "Like I said," Marylou explained for the third time to her disbelieving friend, "I was sitting at my bedroom window and a car drove up in front of my house and somebody threw out a bouquet of flowers and yelled, 'I love you, Marylou,' then he drove off." She didn't tell Lori about how she had lain awake for most of the night, feeling a warm, happy glow just knowing that somebody was thinking about her. Lori would have thought she was jumping the gun.

Both girls jumped as the car behind Lori's honked loudly, signaling them to move on.

"Oh, keep your pants on," Marylou turned around and yelled, then turned back to Lori, looking at her expectantly. "Well, what do you think?"

Lori carefully adjusted her glasses, which had slipped to the end of her nose, and edged her car forward through the intersection before answering. "Why would somebody do that?"

"Why? Obviously, because he likes me!" Marylou exclaimed.

"Yes, but why not just tell you, or ask you out for a date? Why go to all the trouble of driving by your house late at night and throwing flowers on your lawn?"

"Search me." Marylou shrugged. "Maybe whoever did it is shy."

"Do you have *any* idea who it was?" Lori asked.

Marylou shook her head. "I didn't recognize the voice at all. The only clue I have is that he was driving a dark-blue Mustang . . . you know, the hatchback kind."

Lori nodded, concentrating on maneuvering her Chevelle into one of the parking spaces in the Jeffries High School student parking lot. Marylou tried to be patient as Lori tentatively inched the car forward into the parking space, then backed out in order to park the car at precisely the right angle. Lori had gotten her driver's license two months earlier, and Marylou couldn't wait to get hers. It was nice to have a friend who could drive, but Lori's slow, cautious driving made Marylou crazy!

Lori finally got her car into the space, then shut off the engine and faced Marylou. "So, what are you going to do now?" she asked seriously.

"All I have to do is find out who drives a late-model blue Mustang and I'll know who drove by my house and yelled that he loves me!" Marylou said, her excitement rising once again. "After all, he must go to our school, right?"

"Yes, I guess that's true," Lori said thoughtfully, running a hand through her short, dark curly hair. "But you may want to remember that as long as he remains a mystery, you can imagine him as being just perfect. Once you know who he is, you'll kill the fantasy. You know, he'll just be a regular guy."

Marylou thought about what Lori had said, then grinned. "Yeah, but it's pretty hard to have a great relationship with someone you don't know! I guess we'd never fight, but that hardly seems . . ." She looked at Lori curiously, noticing the distant expression on her face. As usual, her friend was lost in thought. "Earth to Lori," Marylou said impatiently. "I hate it when you do that!"

"You hate it when I do what?" Lori asked, gathering up her schoolbooks from the car seat.

"When you drift off into one of your trances," Marylou exclaimed, leaning toward the rearview mirror and giving her hair a final brushing.

"It's called thinking," Lori said dryly. "You might want to try it sometime."

"Ha-ha," Marylou replied. "Well, I *think* we should get into the school building before the bell rings and we both get late slips.

"Seriously, Lori," Marylou continued as they walked into the imposing brick building, "see if you can find out who drives a dark-blue Mustang and I'll do the same, and at lunch we can compare notes." Marylou laughed as she put her arm around her friend. "For today, we're detectives. Our mission is to find

16

my mystery man!" She squeezed Lori's arm. "This is the wildest thing that's happened to me in *ages*!"

Lori folded her arms across her chest and regarded her friend gravely. "I just don't want you to get your hopes up too high. You know, in case nothing comes of this . . ."

Marylou clapped a hand over her friend's mouth, then giggled. "Don't be a party pooper! We've got to look at it this way. The worst thing that can happen is that I'll find out that the guy who threw flowers on my lawn is a real nerd. And frankly, even if he is a nerd, it's still sort of nice to know that at least *somebody* cares enough to pull a stunt like that!"

Both girls jumped as the warning bell rang. "Oh, I've got to run. If I get one more late slip, my mom said she'd confiscate every piece of designer clothing I own!" Marylou exclaimed, running down the hall toward her first class. "I'll see you at lunch," she yelled over her shoulder to Lori.

He could be anybody, Marylou thought delightedly as she slid into her seat in her American history class just as the final bell rang. She looked around the room at her fellow classmates.

He could be sitting in this very room, at this very minute.

She casually looked at each and every guy in the room, but none of them were paying any attention to her. None of them looked as if they were madly in love with her.

Marylou's thoughts were interrupted as the teacher entered the classroom and began a question-and-answer session on the Civil War that demanded all of her attention.

As soon as class was over, Marylou suddenly thought of somebody who might know who owned a dark-blue Mustang. *Tina Lamela knows all the guys in school,* Marylou thought, looking up just in time to see the dark-haired cheerleader leaving the classroom. Marylou ran to catch up with her.

"Tina! Hey, Tina! Could I talk to you for a minute?" Marylou ran to catch up with her pretty, popular classmate.

Tina turned and smiled at Marylou. "Sure, what's up?" She flicked her long curls behind her shoulders.

Marylou smiled gratefully. She and Tina didn't really know each other very well, but Tina had always seemed fairly nice.

"Do you happen to know offhand who drives a late-model dark-blue Mustang?"

Tina frowned. "What happened? Did a dark-blue Mustang run you off the road or something?"

"No," Marylou said hurriedly. "It's nothing like that . . . I . . . uh . . . just saw a car like that with a 'for sale' sign and thought I might check into it," she quickly ad-libbed.

"Oh, are you in the market for a car? 'Cause Jeff Swanson is selling his Volkswagen bug really cheap . . . it's a really good deal."

"Yeah, well, I was really pretty interested in this dark-blue Mustang," Marylou said, feeling her cheeks flush. She hated lying, but she couldn't very well tell Tina the real reason she wanted to know about the blue Mustang's owner.

Tina shrugged. "The only guy I know who owns a blue Mustang like that is Chris Mayfield, and I don't think his is for sale."

Chris Mayfield. Marylou's heart began to beat rapidly. "Okay, well . . . thanks."

"Sure; good luck finding a car!" Tina smiled pleasantly, then headed off toward her next class.

Marylou walked slowly down the hall toward her biology class, her mind whirling. Chris Mayfield! He was a total fox. All the girls thought he was great-looking, with his copper-colored hair and hazel eyes. Chris was president of the junior class, and in charge of the junior class play. Marylou smiled, thinking of the skit Chris had performed last month for a school assembly. He'd been dressed like a magician and had been hysterically funny. Everyone talked about it for days afterwards. At the time, she thought how neat it would be to go out with somebody who had such a great sense of humor. Chris had been in her geology class the year before, and even though she had never gotten to know him, she always thought he was really cool. He was so energetic, always involved in some big project. It was hard to believe that he might be the guy who had driven by her house. *Wait until I tell Lori!* Marylou thought as she hurried to her next class.

It wasn't until lunchtime that she got a chance to talk to Lori. Marylou paid for her lunch and entered the large, noisy cafeteria, immediately spotting Lori at the table near one of the windows where the two girls always ate.

"Wait until you hear!" Marylou burst out with excitement, slipping into the seat across from Lori. "I know who he is!"

"Who?" Lori asked.

"Chris Mayfield!" she answered with a wide grin. "Isn't that fantastic?"

"Chris is really a great guy," Lori smiled approvingly. "You know he's in charge of the junior class play. He's really into drama." Lori frowned suddenly and shoved her eyeglasses up on the bridge of her skinny nose. "But why would a neat guy like Chris stoop to playing games like throwing flowers in the night and yelling 'I love you'?" She looked at Marylou skeptically.

"Maybe because he's a dramatic guy!" Marylou snapped.

Lori shook her head dubiously. "Are you positive it's Chris Mayfield?"

Marylou shrugged. "Tina Lamela told me Chris drives a dark-blue Mustang hatchback, and you know Tina knows everyone who's anyone," Marylou answered.

Lori tilted her head thoughtfully. "Yes, but isn't it possible that somebody else might drive the same kind of car?" Lori asked. "You know, maybe we should just scout out the school parking lot. Maybe we'd even find a blue Mustang out there with flower petals in the floor or on the seat."

Marylou stared at Lori. "What a great idea!" She shook her head in admiration. "I knew there was a reason why I keep you around as my best friend!"

"So, what's my excuse for hanging around you?" Lori asked dryly.

Marylou stuck out her tongue. "Come *on*, let's go outside in the parking lot!"

"I'm eating my lunch!" Lori protested.

Marylou looked at Lori reproachfully. "Lori, what's more important, your appetite or my happiness?"

"Could I have a moment to think about it?" Lori asked, winking at her friend.

"Come on." Marylou hauled Lori out of her chair and guided her toward the exit door that led to the student parking area.

"If it's really Chris Mayfield, it's a shame you didn't try out for a part in the junior class play," Lori commented as the two left the school and walked out into the parking lot. "You should be doing something worthwhile with that amazing memory of yours, anyway, like the debating team or the drama club, instead of baking cakes and making paper flowers for the social committee."

"You sound just like my parents," Marylou laughed. "I don't want to belong to the drama club or the debating team. I like being chairman of the social committee!"

Lori rolled her eyes. "Having a photographic memory is a gift," she replied.

"And it's a gift I put to good use every time I have to take a test!" Marylou pointed out.

"I just think it's a sin that you have such a fantastic memory and you don't make enough use of it," Lori retorted.

"And I think it's a sin that we're wasting the whole lunch period talking about something as stupid as my amazing memory when we could be finding the car that belongs to my secret admirer!" Marylou gazed around the parking lot, searching for blue Mustangs. "Look, there's one!" She grabbed Lori by the arm and tugged her across the parking lot. "Now, act casual," Marylou commanded, glancing at the group of kids who were clustered around the door to the cafeteria, enjoying the sunshine during their lunch hour. "I don't want anyone to know we're snooping around!" As they approached the car, Marylou continued giving instructions to her friend. "Now, as we walk by the car, you look in the passenger window, and I'll look in the driver's window. Look for flower petals, or anything that will give us a clue about who owns that car!"

Lori nodded, and the girls split up, each one inspecting an opposite side of the blue Mustang.

As Marylou passed the driver's side, she stopped and cupped her hands on either side of her face, staring into the interior of the car.

"Oh, that looks real casual," Lori said, peering at her across the top of the Mustang.

Marylou flashed her a quick grin, then looked into the car once again. "I don't see any flower petals, but I do see a football jersey. . . ." Marylou moved to the back of the car and looked in the back window. "I can't quite make out what the number is. . . ." She lay against the back of the car to get a better look. "But I think it's number fifteen," she said excitedly.

"And I see the office secretary looking at us very curiously," Lori said, causing Marylou to jump away from the car. She looked across the parking lot, where there was no one in sight, then looked at Lori accusingly.

Lori shrugged. "It was the best way to get you off the car. Come on, let's get back inside. You've already made me miss lunch. I'm not going to let you make me late for English!"

"Now all I need to find out is who number fifteen is on the football team," Marylou said as they hurried back into the school building. "It can't be Chris Mayfield, because Chris doesn't play football."

"It's Bill Sanders," Lori answered. "I remember because last week I helped Walt print out the football game programs on the computer."

"Bill Sanders!" Marylou sighed incredulously as an image came to mind of the blond senior who was star tackle on the football team. A picture of Bill leaping toward the camera to make a tackle, his blue eyes narrowed in concentration, hung in the hallway outside the gym.

"Just what you need, a macho jock for a boyfriend," Lori quipped.

"Bill isn't just a macho jock," Marylou protested. Lori was unbelievable—she thought all jocks were dumb. "He's always on the honor roll, and he doesn't seem to be a bit stuck on himself like a lot of the guys on the football team."

"That's true," Lori agreed. "I'll admit Bill is of a higher caliber than the usual football player."

"Wow, this is just too good to be true!" Marylou exclaimed as they came to the door of the English classroom.

"Have you noticed either Chris Mayfield or Bill Sanders looking interested in you lately?" Lori asked.

"Shhh!" Marylou hissed. "Do you want the whole English class to know my business?" She moved closer to Lori. "No," she finally answered thoughtfully. "Chris always smiles at me when we pass in the halls, and Bill said hi to me the other day, but other than that, neither of them has given me a sign that he's madly in love with me," she said dryly.

Lori smiled. "There must be some logical way to find out which one of the boys is your secret admirer."

"This doesn't take logic, it takes guts!" Marylou laughed. "I'm just going to have to approach each guy and see if I feel any vibes."

"It always makes me nervous when you talk about all guts and no logic. You always manage to get yourself in trouble with that kind of attitude!" Lori warned.

Marylou laughed. "Now what kind of trouble can I get into by simply trying to discover who loves me?"

Lori shook her head. "I know you, Marylou Watkins, and if trouble is anyplace in the area, you always manage to find it!" Lori pushed her glasses up on the bridge of her nose and wagged her finger at her.

Marylou grinned at her best friend. "I promise —I will stay out of trouble. Come on, we'd better get to our seats. We'll talk more after school," she whispered as they entered the classroom and took their seats. "We've got to come up with a plan," Marylou turned and said to Lori, who sat in the chair behind her.

She turned back around and opened up her English book as their teacher, Mrs. Jackson, entered the room.

"Psst," Lori hissed from behind her. Marylou half turned around and looked at her friend curiously.

Lori nodded toward the row of windows across the room. Marylou looked out the window and her eyes widened—a blue Mustang was pulling into one of the student parking spaces.

I've got to see who's in that car, Marylou thought, leaning over to get a better view. She stared at the Mustang, excitement welling up inside her as she realized that the car was identical to the one that had passed beneath the streetlight on Saturday night.

Marylou leaned closer to the window, unaware that her chair was tipping precariously on two legs beneath her. As she watched, she saw the driver's door swing open and two long, lean, jeans-clad legs emerge.

She heard Lori gasp behind her as the guy stepped out of his car. Marylou instantly recognized his dark good looks. It was Jesse Wilcox! Jesse Wilcox . . . who had his very own band and played at all the school dances! Marylou felt goose bumps of excitement dance up her arms. How could anyone forget the last school dance, where Jesse's band had provided the music? She could remember watching Jesse as he stood in a spotlight and sang a song he had written himself.

I look at you and all I see
Are reflections of what used to be.
How can I forget, what should I do
About the memories of me and you?

She sighed, remembering how romantic, how wonderful she had thought he was. The words to his song had seemed to reach right inside and touch her heart. There was definitely something wonderfully wild and exciting about Jesse Wilcox, rock star to be!

Marylou squealed in surprise as her chair suddenly flew out from beneath her and she landed flat on her rear on the tiled floor.

"Marylou, if you are finished with your astonishing display of gymnastics, we'll begin the lesson for today," Mrs. Jackson said dryly.

"Sorry." Marylou flushed hotly and scrambled back into her seat, hearing her classmates' stifled giggles all around her. Still, neither the embarrassment of falling out of her seat nor Mrs. Jackson's sarcastic reprimand could subdue Marylou's inner excitement. *Chris Mayfield, Bill Sanders, and*

Jesse Wilcox are all popular, great-looking, total hunks! And one of them loves me! she thought, thrilled. *Oh, I can't wait to find out who he is!*

"I can tell all this is going to get you into trouble," Lori whispered from behind Marylou.

"How's that?" Marylou turned slightly in her seat and whispered to her friend. "All I'm going to do is find the guy who loves me. How does that translate into trouble?"

"Marylou, would you and Lori like to share your conversation with the rest of the class?" Mrs. Jackson asked sarcastically.

"Uh . . . I don't think so." Marylou blushed slightly.

"Trouble," Lori hissed, making Marylou bite her lip to keep from giggling. Mrs. Jackson looked at Marylou sternly, then went back to her lesson. Marylou sighed with relief.

Lori is always so serious, she thought to herself. *I'm not going to get into trouble—I'm just going to find my one true love!* With a satisfied smile, she directed her attention to Mrs. Jackson's lesson.

Chapter Three

"Well, it's about time," Lori exclaimed impatiently as Marylou hurried toward her car at the end of school that day.

"Sorry." Marylou smiled apologetically. "I got held up in the hall after school. Jenny Applebee wanted to know what the social committee is planning to do for the French club carnival."

"Well, at least you kept me waiting for something really important," Lori quipped, getting into the car behind the steering wheel while Marylou slid into the passenger seat. "I thought maybe you'd discovered your mystery man.

"You know, I've been thinking about your mystery guy all afternoon," Lori continued, digging into her denim purse for a tissue. "Chris Mayfield. Bill Sanders. Jesse Wilcox. No matter who it turns out to be, you can't lose!"

Marylou grinned. "I can't believe how great they all are myself. It's just incredible that one of those hunks drove by my house and threw the flowers on my lawn."

"I can't believe it either," Lori said frankly, as she started the car.

"Gee, thanks a lot!" Marylou said sarcastically.

"Seriously, it's nothing personal, but look at the situation logically. A guy drives by your house in a blue Mustang and yells he loves you. The next day at school we discover that the three biggest hunks in the whole school drive blue Mustangs. The odds of this happening are . . ." She frowned as if trying to calculate the exact odds.

"I don't know anything about odds; all I know is that this is the most exciting thing that's ever happened to me!" Marylou exclaimed, then frowned thoughtfully. "I just thought of something."

Lori executed a painfully slow left-hand turn.

"What have you thought about?" she asked once the turn was completed.

"Well, I was thinking maybe somebody else has a dark-blue Mustang, somebody other than the three hunks we know about," Marylou said thoughtfully.

Lori shook her head, not taking her eyes off the road. "Of all the students who have student parking permits, there are only three with late-model dark-blue Mustangs, and they're the three guys we've already identified."

"How do you know that?" Marylou asked curiously.

Lori smiled. "After we saw Jesse getting out of the Mustang, I was struck by the idea that there might be several other guys who drove the same kind of car." Lori paused long enough to pull her car into Marylou's driveway. "Anyway, while I was in journalism class this afternoon, I told Mr. Black that I wanted to write an article on the types of cars students drive to school. He suggested I go to the office and research the subject by looking through the file of student parking permits. Naturally, while I was thumbing through the student permits, I just happened to notice everyone who drives a blue Mustang, and there were only three!"

"Thanks, Lori! There are times when your

common sense really helps!" Marylou compli-
mented her friend.

"It's just a matter of deductive thinking,"
Lori said.

"And of course, you are always so logical,"
Marylou laughed.

"Naturally," Lori agreed with a nod. "So,
what are you going to do now?"

Marylou shrugged her shoulders and grinned.
"Tomorrow I'm going to go out of my way to
flirt with all three guys and see how they
react." Marylou's brown eyes gleamed brightly.

"I just don't understand why this guy would
waste time playing games instead of simply
asking you out," Lori said.

"Who cares? All I know is I've been waiting
a long time to have somebody special in my
life, somebody who really cares for me and
who I can really care for."

Lori nodded and Marylou knew her friend
was recalling all the conversations in the past
that the two had shared on this topic.

"Now there's a possibility my dream will
come true," Marylou continued. "I mean, I've
already won half the battle . . . somebody loves
me, and if we're on the right track, that somebody might be one of the most popular guys
in the whole school!" Marylou hugged her

books against her chest as she sighed. "I've got to go for it, Lori!"

Lori looked at her in admiration. "That's what I like about you, Marylou—you never care about what impression you'll make, you just do what you think you have to do."

"Thanks . . . I think." Marylou grinned, knowing Lori had meant it as a compliment. "Do you want to come in for a little while?" she asked, gathering up her books and opening the door.

"No, I can't," Lori said reluctantly. "I have tons of homework. Besides, I promised Mom I'd be home right after school to watch the kids. Mom has a dental appointment."

"The kids" were Lori's three younger sisters, ages five, six, and eight, for whom Lori often babysat.

"Okay, but call me later," Marylou said, getting out of the car.

"Don't I always?" Lori grinned, then pushed her glasses up before she shifted the car into reverse and carefully backed out of Marylou's driveway.

Marylou watched her drive away, then unlocked the front door and stepped inside the quiet house. For as long as she could remember her mom had always been home to greet her after school, but six months ago Mrs.

Watkins had gotten a job as a salesclerk in a clothing boutique. There were times when Marylou missed talking to her mom right after school, but she loved the benefit of her mom's being able to buy clothes at the boutique at a great discount.

Marylou walked into the kitchen and dropped her books on the kitchen table, then grabbed an apple from the fruit basket centerpiece. She bit the apple, crunching loudly as she thought over what Lori had said.

Sure, I worry about what kind of impression I make, she thought, taking another bite of the juicy apple. Normally, she waited for a guy to express his interest in her before she approached him. And even though this particular guy had already expressed his interest, she knew there was a chance she would be rejected by flirting with the wrong two guys first.

Marylou crunched into her apple once again and walked out of the kitchen and down the hallway to her bedroom. As she entered the doorway, her gaze immediately fell on the bouquet of daisies in a vase on her nightstand, and she smiled. "So, what's a little rejection in the quest for true love?" she said aloud. Tomorrow at school, she would start her campaign to find out which guy—Chris, Bill, or

Jesse—was her secret admirer. Her grin widened as she took another bite of her apple.

Marylou dressed with extra-special care the next morning. When she was finished, she looked in her dresser mirror and smiled in satisfaction. Her black corduroy pants hugged her slender legs snugly. Her sweater was one of her favorites, black-and-white checked, with a huge red-and-yellow flower in the center. And the finishing touch was a black hat with a big red bow on it.

"You are hot stuff," she said to her reflection, striking a pose as if she were a high-fashion model. "Too bad you have no cheekbones," she added, sucking in her cheeks to make prominent cheekbones appear. Instead she just looked like a fish.

"Hi, Jesse." She smiled, pretending her image in the mirror was the slim, attractive Jesse Wilcox. "I think we could make hot music together." She grabbed hold of an imaginary guitar and strummed the make-believe strings. She giggled at her own silliness, then sobered and looked at her reflection once again.

"Hi, Bill," she breathed in her sexiest voice. "You can tackle me anytime!" She fluttered her eyelashes flirtatiously, laughing as her hat fell forward on her head.

"Hi, Chris . . . "

"Marylou, Lori is here," her mom called from the kitchen, her voice interrupting Marylou's fantasies.

"Okay, Mom, I'm coming," Marylou answered, sticking her tongue out at her reflection. Then, grabbing the stack of schoolbooks off the top of the dresser, she ran for the front door.

"Have a good day, honey," her mom called from the kitchen.

"Okay; you have one, too," Marylou yelled back. Then she ran out the front door to Lori's car.

"New outfit?" Lori raised her dark-brown eyebrows as Marylou got into the car.

"Yeah, I bought it last week and was saving it for a special occasion. And today is definitely not an ordinary day!" Marylou smiled brightly.

"You still plan to carry out this plan of checking out each of the guys?" Lori asked curiously.

"Sure. Why shouldn't I?" Marylou looked at her friend.

Lori paused a moment before answering. "I don't see why you don't just wait and be patient. Whoever he is will eventually get up enough nerve to ask you out."

"Eventually!" Marylou wailed. "I can't wait that long. I want to know who he is right now!" She looked at Lori suspiciously. "You aren't jealous, are you? I mean, these guys are major hunks, not exactly in Walt's category!"

"Don't be ridiculous," Lori scoffed, bringing her car to an abrupt stop in the school parking lot. She turned off the engine and faced Marylou seriously. "Walt may not be in the major hunk category, but I find him intellectually stimulating!"

Marylou burst out laughing. "Right. I've seen you and Walt in the halls, hanging all over each other and sneaking those long, passionate kisses. Is that what you call intellectual stimulation?"

Lori blushed bright red. "Sometimes you can be so juvenile, Marylou," she retorted, dropping her keys into her purse and getting out of the car.

"Oh, come on, Lori. You make out in the halls and *I'm* juvenile." Laughing, Marylou got out of the car and ran to catch up with Lori. "Anyway, I just hope I don't look too stupid flirting with Chris, Jesse, and Bill."

"Well, at least it won't be the first time you've done something dumb," Lori replied.

"Gee, thanks. I can always count on you for encouragement and support," Marylou said sarcastically.

Lori smiled and linked arms with Marylou as the two walked into school. "Look at it this way: No matter how many weird things you do, you'll always have me as a friend."

"I'm really touched." Marylou grinned as she held open the front door of the school for Lori. They were greeted by the noise of lockers slamming and kids yelling and laughing.

"Have you decided which guy you're going to start with?" Lori asked as they stopped in front of their lockers.

"No. Whoever I see first is the one I'll flirt with first," Marylou said casually.

Lori rolled her eyes. "As usual, I see a lot of thought has gone into this wild scheme of yours. Well, if you're really serious about all this, I see one of your potential guys right now."

"Who? Where?" Marylou's voice rose a full octave higher.

Lori didn't answer, but instead pointed over Marylou's shoulder toward the school courtyard.

Marylou slowly turned around and followed the direction of Lori's index finger. Outside the large window opposite the locker, Marylou could see a group of kids gathered in the small, attractive courtyard. Then suddenly she spotted him, looking wonderfully handsome in the bright sunshine, and her heart began to flutter nervously. Smiling confidently at Lori, Marylou headed outside to where Jesse Wilcox stood, as if he had nothing to do all day but wait for her.

Chapter Four

What am I going to say to him? What am I going to do? Marylou wondered frantically as she walked to the courtyard. She walked around the small fishpond and stood hesitantly near Jesse and his group of friends.

He's so good-looking, Marylou marveled, admiring the way his worn jeans fit his lean legs snugly, and how his leather jacket made him look exciting and sort of dangerous.

Marylou adjusted her hat to a rakish angle and smiled her sexiest smile as Jesse looked over at her. She felt her heart pound frantically as a slow, lazy smile crossed his handsome face.

Marylou's heart sank as the bell rang. *Rats! I was just getting warmed up*, she thought, watching as Jesse and his friends walked to the entrance of the school. As they reached the door, Jesse turned around and gazed directly at Marylou. She felt her heart skip a beat as he smiled at her. Then he winked at her and left the courtyard.

Marylou stared after him in amazement. *Oh, he's so sexy!* She hugged her purse tightly against her chest and sighed deeply. It had to be him, she just knew it. He had to be the one who had driven by her house. *Jesse Wilcox loves me*, she thought, stepping backward. She squealed suddenly, feeling the shock of cold water on her feet. She looked down only to see that she had stepped directly into the fishpond. She frowned as she heard a tapping noise, and turned around to see Lori looking out the window that faced the courtyard. She grinned and shrugged her shoulders as Lori shook her head and rolled her eyes in disbelief. Marylou stepped out of the fishpond and went back into school, trying to ignore the way her shoes squish-squashed with each step she took.

"Honestly, Marylou, how could you forget about the fishpond?" Lori asked as the two walked down the hallway together.

"Who thinks about fishponds at a time like that? Lori, I really think my mystery guy is Jesse!" she said, shaking the excess water off her feet as they came to a stop in front of Marylou's classroom. "Lori, he smiled and winked at me!"

"A smile . . . a wink . . . You're basing your assumption that Jesse is your mystery guy on that?" Lori shook her head. "It sounds pretty weak to me."

Marylou sighed wistfully. "You didn't see the smile or the wink!" When Lori continued to look skeptical, Marylou went on: "Lori, there are times when you can't rely on logic. You just have to go with what your heart says and my heart says Jesse is the one!" Marylou smiled confidently at Lori. "Don't worry, I've got everything under control!"

"It always worries me when you say stuff like that," Lori kidded. "I've got to get to class; I'll talk to you later."

Marylou nodded, watching as Lori hurried away, then she turned and went into her first-period class.

Jesse Wilcox! Marylou said his name over and over again in her mind as her biology teacher lectured on the digestive system of a frog. *Imagine Jesse Wilcox and me as a couple!* She stared blankly at her biology textbook, her mind whirling with images of herself and her new boyfriend.

She had a feeling that a date with Jesse Wilcox would be unlike any date she'd ever been on in her life. Jesse was so exciting—he wouldn't bore her with discussions of skin diseases or be so juvenile as to imitate the sounds of a car crash.

No, she could see her date with Jesse very clearly in her mind. Jesse and his band would be playing a concert in a huge auditorium full of screaming teenage girls. Marylou would have a seat in the very front row. Jesse would come out onstage, looking fine in tight leather pants. He'd grab his guitar and start playing wildly. Then, toward the end of the concert, Jesse would quiet the audience. "And now," he would say, "I'd like to introduce the very special lady in my life. Marylou Watkins, would you please stand up?" Marylou would stand up and a bright spotlight would hit her. "Marylou, I love you," Jesse would say, and every girl in the audience would stare at her with envy.

She shivered at the thought of Jesse choosing her over thousands of other girls. Oh, she would be the envy of every teenage girl in America. Valerie Bertinelli and Eddie Van Halen, move over. Here come Marylou Watkins and Jesse Wilcox!

Marylou continued to be preoccupied with thoughts of Jesse all day. During psychology class, she found herself wondering what she and Jesse would do on a date before he got famous enough to have his own concert. They could always go to a school dance together. Jesse's band would be playing and he would spend most of the night onstage. Marylou would sit next to the band onstage, and Jesse would sing every song especially for her. Then, toward the end of the evening, Jesse would direct the band to play an instrumental. "I want to dance at least one dance with my special girl," he would say, putting down his guitar and leading Marylou out onto the gym floor. The lights would dim as the band played a slow, romantic song. And then, at the end of the dance, Jesse would hold her close, and looking deeply into her eyes, he would kiss her passionately. Oh, it was going to be wonderful having a boyfriend like Jesse Wilcox!

"Personally, I hope Jesse Wilcox isn't your dream guy," Lori said later that afternoon as she and Marylou walked to English class together.

"Why not?" Marylou asked in amazement.

"Jesse isn't exactly in the running for the best student at Jeffries High School; he's in all the remedial classes."

45

"I don't care about that," Marylou scoffed. "It's a well-known fact that school isn't Jesse's number one priority. He's going to be a famous rock-and-roll star."

Lori shot her a pained look. "And he wears all those black T-shirts and leather jackets."

"Well, Walt isn't exactly on the list of best-dressed students, with his corduroy pants and plaid shirts," Marylou retorted.

"At least Walt's hair isn't longer than mine!" Lori returned.

"Walt's kinky hair would look dumb if it were long like Jesse's," Marylou said as they stopped at the door to their English classroom. "You have to admit, Lori, there's something exciting about Jesse. He's such a rebel, and he doesn't care what other people think of him."

"I think that's pretty obvious," Lori said dryly.

"Well, I think it would be great to be Jesse's girlfriend," Marylou said firmly.

Lori pushed her glasses up on the bridge of her nose. "All I know is that today is only the first day of your search for your secret admirer and already you've walked into the middle of a fishpond."

"And if Jesse isn't my mystery guy, then this is just the beginning!" Marylou giggled as Lori groaned loudly. "Come on, we'd better sit down before the final bell rings."

Marylou doodled in her notebook, thinking about everything Lori had said. Sure, Lori was right, Jesse wasn't known as a great student, and his hair was long and he did wear tough-looking clothes. But beneath his rough exterior, Marylou was convinced, he was really romantic and sweet. She reminisced about the way Jesse had smiled at her, about the way his wink had seemed to say that they shared a special secret. *He has to be wonderfully romantic*, she thought. *After all, he drove by my house and yelled "I love you." He threw flowers in my yard . . . or did he?*

Chapter Five

"**M**aybe I should just forget Jesse Wilcox and go on to one of the other blue-Mustang owners," Marylou muttered as she and Lori walked out of the school building. "I haven't seen Jesse since he winked at me in the courtyard the day before yesterday."

"I thought you were sure that Jesse was your mystery guy," Lori said.

"Well, I was pretty positive the other day, but I haven't seen him since then." She frowned. "Maybe he's avoiding me."

Lori shook her head. "I don't think he's been in school for the last couple of days. I haven't seen him at all either, and I always pass him in the halls at least twice a day. Maybe he's been sick," she finished as they reached her car.

"Maybe," Marylou agreed, depressed that two whole days had passed and she still hadn't learned the identity of the mysterious driver.

"Speak of the devil." Lori smiled and pointed back toward the school.

Marylou turned around, her eyes lighting up with excitement as she saw Jesse parking a motorcycle next to the curb. He took off his helmet and got off the bike, then walked into school.

"Lori, take my books home for me, okay?" Marylou quickly threw her schoolbooks into the front seat of Lori's car.

"What about you? What are you going to do?" Lori asked curiously.

Marylou gave Lori a bright, confident grin. "I'm going to persuade my mystery guy to give me a ride home!" She waved to Lori, and started walking back toward the school to the place where Jesse had parked his motorcycle.

When she reached the curb, she stood near Jesse's motorcycle and looked around, pretending that she was waiting for a ride. She hesitated for a moment when she saw Lori drive away. Now, Marylou thought, Jesse had better drive her home, otherwise she had a very long walk ahead of her!

She had been standing there only a few minutes when Jesse came out.

"Well, hello." His dark eyes lit up at the sight of her.

"Hi." Marylou smiled back at him.

"Marylou Watkins, right?" he said with a sexy smile.

"Right!" Marylou's smile widened. He knew her name! That was definitely a good sign!

"So, what are you doing hanging around school after hours?" he asked, looking incredibly cool as he leaned against the seat of the motorcycle.

"Uh . . . I had to stay a few minutes late, and now I'm waiting for my ride." Marylou flushed slightly, hoping this sounded logical.

"How about if I hang out with you while you wait?" Jesse suggested.

"Okay," Marylou agreed. *I'll just stand here and talk to him for a few minutes*, she figured, *then I'll say something about my ride forgetting me and hopefully he'll offer me a ride home.* "So, what are *you* doing hanging around the school after hours?" she asked him.

"I missed the last two days of school and I had some papers due, so I dropped by to turn them in," he explained.

"Were you sick?" she asked, relieved that Lori had been right. He hadn't been trying to avoid her, he'd been absent.

"Yeah . . . sick of school." Jesse let out a low-pitched burst of laughter that managed to sound both mischievous and sexy at the same time. "Actually, my band played at a big battle of the bands in Waverly."

"How did the band do?" Marylou asked curiously.

"Terrific; we placed second. Next year we'll win," he added confidently.

"I thought you drove a blue Mustang," she said as he sat down on the seat of the motorcycle.

Jesse's dark eyes slowly moved over her, from the tip of her head down to her toes, and that incredibly sexy smile once again appeared. "I use my Mustang to carry my musical equipment. So, you've been checking me out, huh?"

Marylou flushed. *If he looks at me like that one more time, I'm going to melt!* She wondered how she could be standing up so straight when her legs felt like jelly. She just stared at Jesse and remained speechless.

Jesse laughed. "Don't worry, it's cool that you've been checking me out. I've been checking you out, too."

"And what have you found out about me?" Marylou asked, wondering where she was getting the nerve from.

Jesse grinned. "That's for me to know and you to find out," he said, getting off his motorcycle and coming to stand close to her. He was standing so close that she could smell a pleasant mixture of minty soap and the leather of the black jacket he was wearing. "I'll tell you one thing," he said softly, reaching out and touching the end of her hair lightly. "I definitely like what I see. You looked cute the other day in the courtyard in that funky black hat with the red bow."

Once again, Marylou's heart fluttered, and she prayed she wouldn't fall flat on her face. She'd never met anyone so fantastic before! This guy could teach Patrick Swayze a thing or two about sex appeal!

Jesse laughed softly, as if aware of the effect he was having on her. "Actually, I heard several things about you," he said, leaning back against the motorcycle and smiling at her lazily. "I heard that you were the girl who got caught last year hiding in the boys' locker room during a football game."

Marylou flushed and mumbled, "That story was drastically exaggerated. Last year I was on the school newspaper staff, and I thought it would be exciting to get an interview with the quarterback during halftime. You know, get his perspective on his own performance during the first half. Unfortunately, the coach came in and thought I was there for less than admirable reasons, and he threw me out. I was penalized with two Saturday detentions, but Mr. Black, the newspaper adviser, convinced the principal to let me off the hook."

Jesse laughed. "I think I've spent half my life in Saturday detentions."

"Doesn't that bother you?" she asked in amazement.

"Nah, it doesn't bother me. If not for my old man, I would have dropped out of school two years ago. But I promised him that I'd at least graduate from high school."

Marylou looked at him in surprise. *We're so different from each other*, she thought. *My friends and I consider school and grades to be pretty important—not one of us has ever dreamed about dropping out of school.* "Aren't you interested in going to college?" she asked.

Jesse looked at her in disbelief. "That's

about the last thing I'd want to do. The day I get my diploma will be the last day I'll spend in school."

"What are you going to do when you graduate?" Marylou asked curiously.

"I'm going to make music," Jesse answered without hesitation. "The guys in the band and I are going to travel. We're already setting up gigs all around the Midwest."

Marylou nodded, although she wasn't sure she knew what he was talking about. "It all sounds really exciting."

"Yeah, we're working on some original numbers so we can eventually cut our own record. Do you want to hear one?"

"Sure," Marylou answered, watching as he pulled a small cassette player from a bag on the back of the motorcycle. He rewound the tape and then played it. He sat down on the motorcycle seat as the sounds of the band filled the air around them. Jesse leaned his head back and closed his eyes, rocking his body slightly with the rhythmic beat of the music.

Gosh, he's so gorgeous, Marylou thought, tapping her foot to the sounds of the music. Although Marylou rarely listened to heavy metal, and she couldn't understand the words, she had to admit the beat was great for dancing. Anyway, she was more interested in looking at Jesse than she was in listening to the music.

"What do you think?" he asked, clicking off the machine as the song came to an end.

"It sounds great and it's really got a good beat," Marylou answered honestly, her heart thudding as loudly as the drums on the tape as Jesse once again stood up and moved very close to her.

"So, you like my music?" he asked, his soft voice causing her stomach muscles to jump and twitch nervously.

"Sure, it was real good," Marylou answered faintly, then laughed self-consciously and took a step back from him. *He's so sexy, and he knows it,* she thought as she watched him smile. *He also scares me just a little bit—he's so smooth!*

"You know what else I heard about you?" Jesse said, moving closer to her once again.

"What?" Marylou breathed, realizing her mouth was totally dry. He was standing so close to her, she could feel his warm breath on her face.

"I heard you can look at a page and memorize it immediately."

"That's true," Marylou said softly.

"Wow, that's something else," Jesse said,

looking at her in admiration. "You could memorize the words to the top ten hits in no time at all."

"Well, yes, I guess I could," Marylou answered.

"Are you sure your ride is coming for you?" Jesse looked down at his watch. "It's getting pretty late."

"Gee, I guess maybe my friend forgot about me. She's sort of flaky," Marylou said, knowing Lori would forgive her for one little lie.

"Come on, I'll take you home," Jesse said, taking his helmet and putting it on. As he buckled it beneath his chin, Marylou admired the way his long, dark hair hung out from beneath the edge of the helmet. "Come on," he urged her. "You can't hang around the school all night. It's bad for your health."

"Okay," Marylou agreed, not moving from her position on the curb. *This is great,* she thought, unable to believe her luck. *I'll get on the back of his motorcycle and I'll snuggle up to him.*

"Well?" Jesse started up his motorcycle with a roar. "I can't very well take you home if you won't hop on."

Marylou looked at him hesitantly. "What about a helmet?" she asked. "Isn't it important that I wear one, too?"

"I don't have an extra one," he yelled above

the throbbing of the motorcycle engine. "Come on, don't worry about it. I'm a great driver." There was a touch of impatience in his voice.

Don't worry about it? Marylou looked at him blankly. *Why doesn't he offer me his helmet?* she wondered. *Doesn't he care about my safety? This is my dream guy, the guy who loves me so much he drove by my house and threw flowers on my lawn?*

With a nervous smile, Marylou climbed on behind him, grateful that she had worn slacks to school that day instead of one of her short skirts.

She shyly put her arms around Jesse's waist, hoping he wouldn't pop a wheelie or peel out of the lot at top speed. She knew what she was doing wasn't right, but she figured it would be okay to ride without a helmet just this once.

Jesse turned around and grinned at her. "So, where do you live?"

"Where do I live?" Marylou looked at him blankly.

"Yeah, you know . . . what's your address . . . where's your house?" he asked, his fingers drumming on the seat.

Shocked at his question, Marylou practically fell off the motorcycle seat. "You mean you don't know where I live?"

"No, but if you'll tell me, I'll take you home!" Jesse exclaimed, turning around to look at her as if she were crazy.

Feeling a keen disappointment, Marylou slowly swung her leg off the seat. *You can't be him! My special guy would already know where I live,* she thought, staring at Jesse in confusion. She'd been so sure, but obviously she'd been wrong. How embarrassing! But since he wasn't the one, it certainly wasn't worth risking a motorcycle ride without a helmet.

"What are you doing *now*?" asked Jesse with obvious annoyance.

"I-I just remembered that, uh, my friend said to wait, she might be a little late," Marylou mumbled.

"I think you're the flake, not your friend!" Jesse exclaimed. Revving up his engine, he took off, the motorcycle screeching as he pulled away from the curb.

Marylou choked in the cloud of exhaust and dirt that hovered in the air behind him. She watched the motorcycle disappear up the street, not at all sorry he wasn't the guy she was looking for. True, he was incredibly sexy, but they were so different, and a romance would never have worked out between them.

Besides, he obviously couldn't care less about things like safety!

She sighed and started walking away from the school. Thanks to Jesse and her own impulsive behavior, she had a thirty-minute walk home—plenty of time to come up with a new scheme to find her mysterious admirer!

Chapter Six

Marylou peeked around the corner, gazing at Bill Sanders, who was standing at his locker just a few feet away from where she was hiding. As he turned and looked in her direction, she jumped back around her side of the corner, biting her bottom lip as she banged her funny bone on the locker behind her. "Darn, darn, darn!" she muttered, holding her throbbing elbow with her hand.

After her fiasco the day before with Jesse, she was determined to go a little slower with Bill and Chris. She was going to spy on them first and see what she could find out about them.

She frowned as she remembered Jesse's parting words to her. A flake. He had actually called her a flake! She leaned against the wall, out of Bill's sight, thinking about Jesse Wilcox. He was the flake, actually thinking she would be stupid enough to ride home on the back of his motorcycle without a helmet. He drove his motorcycle like a total maniac!

Actually, she was sort of relieved that her mystery guy was not Jesse Wilcox. True, he was really great-looking and sexy beyond belief, not to mention a great musician, but his wild streak definitely made her a little nervous. *Maybe Bill was more her type,* she thought as she peeked around the corner again, watching him remove a stack of books from his locker. He was certainly good-looking, although in a much different way than Jesse. Bill had short-cropped blond hair and a square face with a firm jawline and a cleft in his chin, which deepened when he smiled. Jesse's face was dark and mysterious, while Bill's was open and friendly. Bill was bigger and more muscular than Jesse, too.

"What are you doing?" Lori's voice blared unexpectedly in Marylou's ear, startling her so that she jumped in surprise. She lost her balance and stumbled forward and right

61

into Bill's broad back! The force of her body pushed the handsome blond football player headfirst into his open locker. Marylou cringed as she heard his head make contact with metal.

"Oh, I'm *so* sorry!" Marylou blushed as she regained her balance and helped Bill straighten up.

"That's all right." Bill said, turning around to face her and rubbing his forehead where a red mark was beginning to appear. He grinned when he glanced at her, causing the cleft in his chin to dance attractively. "No major harm done."

"I'm so clumsy sometimes," Marylou murmured with embarrassment, slamming his locker door shut for him nervously.

"Ouch!" Bill yelped, and to Marylou's horror she saw that she had slammed the locker door on his sleeve.

"Oh, gosh . . . hold still, I'll get you loose," Marylou gasped, grabbing his firmly muscled arm and tugging.

"Wait a minute . . . you're gonna rip . . . "

Rrrrrip. There was a loud, tearing sound.

". . . my shirt," Bill finished his sentence.

Marylou looked at him with wide, horror-filled eyes. His arm was now loose, but the sleeve of his shirt hung in shreds.

"Oh, I'm so sorry." Marylou felt tears pool in her eyes, and fervently wished she could reverse the course of events to avoid this awful moment. This boyfriend search had been nothing but trouble!

"It's okay—I know you didn't mean it." Bill laughed and took a step back from her. "I'll just have to watch out for you in the future—you're dangerous!"

Marylou backed away from him. "I'm *really* sorry, Bill." She looked from the red mark on his forehead to his ripped shirt sleeve. "I'll buy you a new shirt," she muttered. She turned and ran back around the corner of the corridor, where Lori was waiting for her, her hand clasped over her mouth to stifle her giggles.

"Shut up and don't say a word!" Marylou exclaimed, knowing her face was beet-red. "I can't believe this, I just can't believe this! I only wanted to spy on him, and instead I practically break his skull and rip his shirt." She moaned. "Even if he was my mystery guy, he probably hates me now. I practically killed him!"

"Don't be so dramatic," Lori countered, unsuccessfully trying to hide a smile of amusement. "At least he was laughing throughout the whole ordeal."

"Yeah, right. But now I'll never know if he smiles at me because he loves me, or because he's remembering the way I practically maimed him for life!" She looked at Lori accusingly. "And it's all your fault!"

"*My* fault!" Lori squeaked in surprise, her glasses sliding down to the tip of her long nose. "What did *I* do?" She shoved her glasses back up, gazing at Marylou soberly.

"You snuck up behind me while I was sneaking up on Bill!" Marylou glared at Lori, then suddenly began to giggle as she saw the humor of the whole situation. She remembered the look on Bill's face—the scene had been like something out of an old Marx brothers movie! And Lori was right that Bill hadn't stopped smiling the whole time.

"Well, at least Bill is a better candidate for a boyfriend than Jesse," Lori said as they continued down the hall. "Although, personally, I'm really hoping your guy ends up being Chris."

"Why?" Marylou asked curiously.

Lori shrugged. "Chris is so cute, and he's not a dumb jock," Lori explained.

"Bill isn't a dumb jock!" Marylou protested. "He's a smart jock. And he's really cute, too. He's got the cutest cleft in his chin."

"Oh, well, that's a really important consideration," Lori said sarcastically. "Marylou, I thought you wanted to become involved in a *serious* relationship."

"I'm not basing a relationship solely on that," Marylou protested. She lowered her voice and continued thoughtfully, "Lori, I'm already half in love with my secret admirer. Anyone who would drive by my house and yell 'I love you' and throw flowers on my lawn has got to be the boy of my dreams!"

Lori looked at Marylou seriously. "I just hope you aren't disappointed."

"How can I be disappointed? I just know I'm going to fall madly in love with my mystery man," she said confidently as Lori merely shook her head.

Marylou hurried out of her fifth-period class. Her arms were filled with books and she was hoping she would have time to stop at her locker and drop off some of them before her next class. But before she could reach her locker, the warning bell rang.

"Darn," she muttered, picking up her pace as she turned the corner of the corridor, hurrying to get to her class before the final bell rang. "Ooomph!" She gasped for air as she collided with a hard, big body, sending books and papers flying everywhere.

"Oh, I'm so sorry," she murmured, not even bothering to look up as she scurried around to collect all her papers and books.

"I think I should buy you a sign that says 'Accident Waiting to Happen'!"

Marylou looked up to see Bill looming over her with an amused expression on his face. "You are definitely hazardous to my health!"

Oh, just great, Marylou thought, picking up the last of the papers. *You can definitely write Bill off your list.* She could feel a hot blush cover her face. She stood up and grinned at Bill, trying to make light of the embarrassing situation. "Actually, I've been paid a lot of money by the Westside Cougars to see that our star tackle is injured for Saturday night's game," she said impulsively, knowing the Jeffries High School Tigers and the Westside High School Cougars were bitter rivals and were playing their first game of the season on Saturday night.

Bill's grin widened, causing the cleft in his chin to deepen. "One more of these encounters and I'd say you'll have earned your money!"

"I really am sorry." Marylou apologized once again, handing him several of his papers that she had picked up off the floor. "I seem to have developed a terrible case of the clumsies today."

"I know what you mean. I have days like

that, too." Bill's blue eyes gazed at her with open interest. "Unfortunately, I usually develop my case of clumsies in the middle of an important football game. Put a pair of cleats on my feet and I end up tripping myself instead of tackling the members of the other team's offensive line."

Marylou laughed, her heart beating rapidly in her chest. Bill was so nice. *Is he the one?* she wondered, admiring his clean-cut handsomeness.

"Hey, do you like football?" Bill asked suddenly.

"Oh, sure," Marylou lied effortlessly. She really didn't know if she liked football or not. She'd never even been to one of the high school games and she really didn't know anything about it. But that wasn't something you admitted to the team's star tackle!

"Great!" Bill smiled at her with approval. "You know, after the big game this Saturday night there's a dance." Both he and Marylou jumped as the final bell rang. "Oh no, I'm late . . . the coach is gonna kill me! I've got to go . . . I'll talk to you later," Bill called as he turned and ran down the hallway.

"Bill . . . wait!" Marylou called frantically after him. "What about Saturday night? What were you going to say?"

Bill turned around and ran backward. "Will you go to the dance with me Saturday night after the game?" he yelled.

"Yes," Marylou answered breathlessly, then she yelled louder. "Yes!" Her heart swelled with happiness as Bill disappeared from sight. The first step had been accomplished: She had a date with Bill Sanders! At this point, she almost didn't care if he was her mystery man or not. He was such a great guy. She hurried down the hallway, not even minding that she was late for her next class.

Chapter Seven

Marylou dressed very carefully for her date on Saturday night. Bill had finalized the plans for their date the day before at school, telling her he would meet her after the game at the entrance of the locker room and they would go to the dance from there.

"I figure it will be safer for me to spend the evening with you than to take a chance of running into you unexpectedly," he'd teased, making her laugh as she remembered their previous encounters at school.

She smiled now at her reflection in the mirror. It had been a long time since she had been this excited about a date, but each time she had talked to Bill, she had liked him a little bit more.

She studied her reflection, pleased with the way she looked. She'd talked her mom into an advance on her allowance so that she could buy a new outfit from the boutique. The lavender denim skirt hugged her hips, then flared into a full skirt. Her pink-and-lavender-striped knit top was tucked in to show off her slim waist. She turned as she heard a knock on her bedroom door. "Come in," she yelled, smiling as her mom entered the room.

"Oh, honey, you really look pretty!" Mrs. Watkins smiled at Marylou.

"Thanks, Mom." Marylou nervously smoothed her skirt and turned away from the mirror.

"So, why isn't this young man coming to pick you up for your date?" her mom asked, sitting down on the edge of Marylou's bed.

"Remember, I told you. Bill's a football player, and he's playing in tonight's game. Nighttime football games are supposedly really exciting, with all the flood lights shining on the field. So, I'm going to the game with Lori, then Bill is taking me to the dance afterward," Marylou explained.

Mrs. Watkins nodded, then smiled, "Don't you think it's about time to throw away these flowers?" She gestured at the vase of daisies sitting on Marylou's nightstand.

Marylou walked over and touched the browning, dying daisies. "I suppose I really should throw them out," she began hesitantly, then grinned. "But I think I'll leave them here just a little bit longer. It makes me feel good just to look at them."

"I can see why. It's always a nice feeling knowing someone loves you." Mrs. Watkins smiled. "Especially when that someone is not your parents."

Marylou smiled. "Being loved by your parents is really nice." She gently touched the daisies with the tip of her finger. "But this . . . this is really special."

"Do you really think this Bill is the one who gave you the flowers?" Marylou's mother asked.

"I hope so," Marylou said fervently. "I've already struck out with Jesse. That means there's a fifty-fifty chance that it's Bill."

"And a fifty-fifty chance that it's not Bill," her mom reminded her with a grin.

"Hopefully I'll know for sure tonight," Marylou replied. "Bill will probably say or do something tonight that will let me know for sure if he's the one."

"And if he isn't?" Mrs. Watkins asked.

Marylou shrugged and grinned. "Then I'll know for sure that my mystery guy is Chris Mayfield. But in the meantime, I'll enjoy being with Bill. He's a great guy—not like Jesse."

"Jesse . . . Chris . . . Bill." Mrs. Watkins threw her hands up with a burst of laughter. "This teenage romance stuff is much too confusing for me!"

Marylou laughed. "With every day that passes it's getting less confusing. At least I've narrowed it down to two guys, and hopefully after tonight I'll know exactly who my secret admirer is!" She cocked her head to one side, hearing the sound of a car horn. "That must be Lori." She grabbed her denim jacket from her chair.

"I hope you girls have a good time," Mrs. Watkins said as she and Marylou left the bedroom. "And I hope you have a really good time with Bill, but don't forget your midnight curfew."

"We will, I will, and I won't!" Marylou giggled as she flew out the front door with a wave goodbye.

"Hey, you look great! New outfit?" Lori greeted Marylou as she got into the car.

"Yeah. Thanks. I spent all of next month's

allowance and all my savings on it." Marylou smoothed down her skirt after she slid into the car. "I'm hoping that my date with Bill tonight will make having no spending money next month worth it "

"I hope you're right, because I can't imagine you giving up shopping for a whole month," Lori drawled as she backed out of Marylou's driveway.

"Ah yes, but true love is worth any sacrifice." Marylou sighed and fluttered her eyelashes dramatically.

"I think I'm going to be sick," Lori replied dryly, grinning as Marylou giggled. "I want you to know that the only reason I'm going to this game tonight is because you asked me to come with you," Lori said. "Personally, I think football games are totally barbaric!"

"And I appreciate your going with me." Marylou grinned at her best friend, then wrinkled her brow in a frown. "I just hope I'll understand football. I'd like to be able to talk to Bill tonight about the game and not make a total fool of myself. Whenever Dad turns the ball games on at home, Mom and I head for the nearest mall for a couple hours of shopping."

"Well, basically, one team has the ball and

tries to get to the opposite side of the field, and the other team tries to stop them, and vice versa."

Marylou smiled at her friend brightly. "Well, that sounds easy enough!"

Once the girls had found seats on the home team bleachers and the football game had gotten under way, Marylou realized that the game of football was not as easy to understand as Lori had led her to believe. There were first downs, illegal motions, clipping, and offside calls. The only thing Marylou knew for certain was that Bill looked totally fantastic in his uniform!

"What's happening? I couldn't even see who had the ball," Marylou complained after a particularly confusing play.

"That play is called a quarterback sneak," Lori explained. As she saw the look of confusion on Marylou's face, she pulled a small notebook out of her purse and began to write furiously.

"What are you doing?" Marylou asked, watching player number 15 out of the corner of her eye.

"I'm making you a list. . . . In this column are the key offensive plays, and in this column are the key defensive plays. Bill is defense, so he'll be involved in these plays." Lori handed Marylou the sheet of paper.

"How do you know all this?" Marylou asked curiously.

Lori smiled sheepishly. "Walt likes football."

Marylou laughed in delight. "Walt the computer freak has a secret passion to be a jock?"

"No, he just likes watching football," Lori replied haughtily.

Marylou grinned, then studied the paper Lori had given her. After looking at it for a few minutes, she glanced up at the field, and frowned as she saw Bill sitting on the bench talking to the head cheerleader, Michelle Osgood. "That's the third time tonight that Michelle has cozied up to Bill. What does she think she's doing?" Marylou muttered.

"She's probably just asking him something about the game so she can lead the next cheer," Lori replied.

"I suppose," Marylou said, still unhappy with the way Michelle was standing so close to Bill, whispering in his ear.

At halftime Lori and Marylou made their way through the crowd and stood in line at the concession stand.

"Isn't this exciting?" Marylou said to Lori.

"Actually, it's a lot more fun than I thought

it would be," Lori admitted. "And the smell of that popcorn has been driving me crazy!"

"It does smell good," Marylou agreed, waving to a girl from her math class. "In fact," she continued with excitement, "the whole night smells good!" And it was true; the autumn night air smelled crisp and fresh, mingling with the scent of freshly popped popcorn and roasting peanuts.

Marylou watched as a group of cheerleaders walked by them. She noticed with a twinge of envy how cute Michelle Osgood looked in the blue-and-gold cheerleading uniform.

"You know, I've never been sorry I didn't try out for cheerleader until tonight," Marylou said thoughtfully.

"Why do you suddenly have a desire to be a cheerleader?" Lori asked as they moved closer to the concession stand.

"It must be a lot of fun to be down there on the field right next to the players," Marylou said wistfully, imagining herself in a cute cheerleading outfit, exchanging flirtatious words with Bill.

"You've got one of your dopey looks on your face," Lori commented, peering at Marylou.

"I do not," Marylou said defensively, grateful that they had reached the concession stand and it was their turn to order.

Within minutes Marylou and Lori were making their way back through the crowd toward their seats in the bleachers, each carrying a giant tub of popcorn and a large cola. As the kickoff for the second half took place, Marylou gazed at Bill. The shoulder pads made his broad shoulders look even bigger, and his waist and hips looked slim and well-formed. Marylou was amazed at how gracefully Bill moved for such a big guy. She shivered with excitement. After the game, Bill would move just as gracefully with her in his arms, dancing across the gym floor. She closed her eyes, imagining how his strong muscles would feel beneath her hands as she clasped him around his neck.

"What happened?" Marylou's eyes flew open as she was jolted from her thoughts by the sudden roar of the crowd. Lori shrugged in bewilderment, and Marylou looked back to the field where the referee was making some funny gestures and yelling "Number fifteen."

"Hurray!" Marylou jumped up and cheered. After all, the referee was yelling Bill's number, so he must have done something great!

"Hey, sit down! Are you sitting in the wrong bleachers or what?" the man behind her yelled.

"Of course not!" Marylou said indignantly. "I'm cheering for Jeffries High School. Number fifteen is my date tonight!" She returned the man's glare.

"Oh, yeah? Well, your boyfriend just got penalized fifteen yards for a personal foul. Do you always cheer when he screws up?" the man returned.

Marylou looked at him in confusion. "You mean Bill did something wrong?"

The man sighed in exasperation and rolled his eyes. "Yeah, he did something wrong! I'll never understand why they allow women to come to football games!"

Marylou started to say something about male chauvinists, but stopped as Lori yanked her back down onto the seat. "Don't make a scene!" Lori hissed.

"I wasn't going to make a scene," Marylou protested, smoothing down her skirt in frustration. "I was simply going to explain that I made a mistake and he's a male chauvinist pig!"

"Then it's a good thing I yanked you down when I did, otherwise there might have been more violence here in the stands than down there on the field!" Lori teased Marylou. "And you wouldn't want to meet Bill later with a black eye or a bloody nose that you got in a fight."

Marylou giggled. "Somehow I don't think Bill would be surprised if I did."

The rest of the game passed quickly, with Bill more than making up for his mistake. During the last quarter of the game, Bill managed to tackle the opposing team's quarterback three times. the man behind Marylou patted her on the back and told her what a great guy her boyfriend was. The game ended with a score of 21 to 14 in favor of Jeffries High School. Both Marylou and the man behind her cheered loudly when a booming voice announced over the loudspeaker that Bill Sanders had been chosen as the game's most valuable player.

"Call me first thing in the morning and tell me about your date with Bill," Lori demanded as the two of them walked toward the exit gate.

"You know I will." Marylou smiled. "And thanks again for coming to the game with me tonight."

"I really haven't changed my opinion about football being a barbaric game, but I have to admit there is something contagious about the whole atmosphere." Lori smiled at Marylou. "I'll talk to you tomorrow!" She waved and headed for her car.

Marylou watched her go, happy to have a friend as dependable as Lori was. She could be irritating, with her dry sense of humor and her intellectual way of looking at things. She didn't have a lot of friends because most kids thought she was sort of nerdy, but Marylou knew Lori would do anything for her, and in turn, Marylou would do anything for Lori. Though Lori sometimes acted sort of superior, Marylou knew Lori was painfully shy and insecure.

When Lori was out of sight, Marylou turned and started walking toward the school door that led to the corridor where the locker rooms were. There were several girls clustered near the door, obviously also waiting for their dates to get changed.

Marylou adjusted the collar of her denim jacket with nervous excitement as the door opened, but the guy coming out of the school wasn't Bill. Boy after boy came out and Marylou watched as the girls claimed their dates and disappeared in the direction of the gym for the dance.

Finally, Marylou was the only girl left waiting at the door.

He'll be out any minute, she assured herself, watching the door steadily. *He's probably just taking extra time changing his clothes because he wants to look really good for his date with me. By the time I count to ten, he'll come through that door,* she thought. *One . . . two . . . three . . .*

By the time she had counted to ten three times, she was beginning to worry. *What if he forgot our date?* she wondered. *What if he changed his mind about wanting to go out with me? Maybe I was supposed to meet him by the gym door instead of by the locker room door?* Marylou's frown deepened. *Maybe he really was mad when I knocked him down at the lockers and he decided to stand me up.* Marylou felt the first stirrings of anger.

Nobody stands up Marylou Watkins, she thought indignantly. *The least he could have done was come out here and face me like a man and tell me he decided not to take me to the dance!* She eyed the door thoughtfully. She could go inside and just stand in the hallway. At least she wouldn't be standing out alone in the cold.

Her decision made, Marylou straightened her shoulders and pushed on the door. As it swung inward, she heard a grunt and felt the door hit something solid. She stepped back in surprise and Bill came out, rubbing his nose and groaning slightly.

He dropped his hand and grinned at her ruefully. "I made it through four quarters of a tough football game without a single injury. Before I've even officially started my date with you, you've managed to break my nose!"

"Oh, no! Is . . . is your nose broken?" Marylou looked at him in horror.

His grin widened. "No, it's not broken, just slightly mashed."

"That's good." Marylou breathed a sigh of relief. "I mean, it's bad that it's mashed, but it's good that it's not broken." She smiled at him shyly, noticing for the first time how handsome he looked at that moment. His hair was damp and he smelled fresh, as if he had just stepped out of a shower. He was wearing jeans and a blue striped sweater that showed off his broad shoulders and complemented his blue eyes.

"Did you think I'd forgotten our date?" he asked, taking her hand as they walked toward the gymnasium.

"I have to admit, it did cross my mind," Marylou answered.

"How could I forget a date with the girl who practically broke my arm, ripped my shirt, and flattened my nose?" He grinned down at her. "Just promise me one thing."

"What?" Marylou looked up at him with a smile.

"Promise me you won't break my foot or anything like that when I dance with you."

Marylou giggled and shook her head. "Okay, I promise." She felt her heart thud loudly as Bill smiled down at her again and squeezed her hand. *I hope he's the one,* she thought, *because I could really get to like him!* She giggled suddenly. *If I don't kill him first!*

Chapter Eight

"Oh, wow, the gym really looks great!" Bill commented as he and Marylou walked through the doors and into the gym, which had been transformed into a country autumn scene. The walls were hung with huge posters depicting pumpkin patches and scarecrows. Bales of hay were stacked in all four corners of the gym, providing places for the kids to sit and talk.

"Yeah, it does. I'm head of the social committee and we worked all day yesterday," Marylou said proudly.

"You did a great job," Bill said, as he led

her toward the refreshment table. "Come on, let's get something to drink."

As they made their way across the room, Bill was greeted with congratulations on being chosen the most valuable player of the game.

"I feel like I'm with some kind of celebrity or something," Marylou teased as they each took a paper cup full of apple cider.

"Ah, it's no big deal." Bill's face flushed slightly. "I had to redeem myself after I committed that personal foul."

Marylou smiled up at him, touched by the faint blush on his face. *It's nice that he's so modest,* she thought. "What exactly did you do? I sort of missed that part of the game," she said, remembering how she had thought Bill had done something good.

Bill's blush deepened. "The tackle from the other team was goading me through the whole game, you know, making raunchy comments. I should have ignored him. I shouldn't have let him get to me, but he did." Bill paused and took a sip of his apple cider, then grinned at her sheepishly. "So, I lost my cool, grabbed his face mask and threw him down in the dirt, and bingo . . . a fifteen-yard penalty. It was a dumb move on my part."

"You more than made up for it throughout the rest of the game," Marylou said, finishing her cider and throwing away her paper cup. "I really liked that screen thing you did for that last touchdown!"

"Thanks." Bill looked at her strangely, making her wonder if she'd gotten mixed up. Was a screen an offensive play or a defensive play? She tried to recall the list of plays Lori had made for her. Before Bill had a chance to reply, Michelle Osgood ran over to him and grabbed him by the arm.

"Oh, Bill, you were terrific tonight," she exclaimed, squeezing Bill's arm tightly and smiling up at him. Marylou felt an intense pang of jealousy as Bill smiled back at the pretty cheerleader.

"Thanks, Michelle." He looked over at Marylou. "Marylou, are you ready for a dance?"

"Sure," Marylou replied happily, allowing Bill to lead her out onto the dance floor. She was pleased to see that Bill was a really good dancer. Bill moved lightly on his feet, looking like he was very comfortable and at ease with his body. Marylou loved to dance, but she particularly loved to dance when she had a good partner. So many of the guys she had dated either moved like robots on the dance floor or looked like they were going through painful convulsions.

One dance led to another and another until

finally the disc jockey played a slow song. Bill moved close to Marylou and put his arms around her waist. Marylou reached up to put her arms around his broad chest. As she lay her head softly against the front of his sweater, she could hear the faint thump-thump of his heartbeat. She tilted her head back and smiled up at him. "You're a very good dancer."

Bill drew back from her a little bit so he could see her face. "I've had a lot of practice. I have an older sister who always forced me to be her dance partner so she could practice. At the time I hated it, but now I'm glad I did it so I can dance without embarrassing myself."

"How old is your sister?" Marylou asked, smiling at the image of a young Bill dancing with an older girl.

"Karen is twenty-two," he answered.

"Do you have any other brothers or sisters?" Marylou asked. It suddenly seemed important that she know everything about him.

"No," he said, laughing. "But one is more than enough!"

"I always wished I had a sister or brother," Marylou admitted, "you know, somebody to share secrets with."

Bill laughed. "If I told Karen any of my secrets, she'd blackmail me!" Then he added, "Actually, Karen and I are pretty close. In fact, I often ask her for advice. She just got married a couple of months ago and lives near our house."

Marylou nodded and leaned against him. *Maybe it was his sister's idea to throw flowers on my lawn,* she thought. *If he is the one who did it,* she reminded herself.

After the slow dance, she and Bill headed for the bales of hay that had been set up for people to sit on.

"So, tell me something about Marylou Watkins," Bill said once they were seated beside each other, surrounded by stacked bales of hay.

Marylou shrugged and grinned. "There isn't much to tell. What do you want to know?"

"I don't know. . . . The only things I really know about you are that you're dangerous with doors, you're pretty rough on shirts, and you like to rearrange noses," he said teasingly.

Marylou giggled. "At least I didn't mash any of your toes while we were dancing!"

"That's true," Bill laughed, "and for that I am grateful." He gazed into her eyes, and Marylou knew she had a stupid smile on her face. Suddenly she blurted out, "I love pizza and spaghetti, my favorite color is purple, and when I was thirteen I was madly in love with Rob Lowe. There, now you know everything about me!"

"Somehow, I don't think that's even the beginning," Bill laughed. "I love pizza too, but I really love tacos. My favorite color is blue, and when I was thirteen years old . . . " Bill paused a moment thoughtfully, then grinned. "When I was thirteen years old I thought all girls were alien life forms!"

Marylou laughed. "And do you still think all girls have cooties?"

"Not all girls." He leaned close to her, so close that she could feel his soft breath on her cheek. "You look pretty okay to me," he said softly, making Marylou's heart pound as if it were caught in her throat.

"That's good," she uttered breathlessly. *Kiss me*, she thought. She leaned forward to encourage him, but as she shifted positions, they accidentally bumped into the bales of hay behind them. Just as Bill's lips were about to touch hers, the small bale on top tipped over and fell directly on them. As it hit, the string that bound the hay together burst, and hay spilled all over them.

Coughing and laughing wildly, they both jumped up, brushing hay from their hair and clothes.

"Are you kids okay?" Mr. Roland, their math

teacher and one of the dance chaperones, hurried over to them, a worried frown creasing his face.

"Yeah, we're fine," Bill laughed, pulling a handful of hay from the shoulder of his sweater. "I sort of feel like the Scarecrow from *The Wizard of Oz!*"

Marylou laughed and shook the hay out of her hair. "Yeah, and the Wicked Witch of the West just stomped the stuffing out of us."

Mr. Roland, satisfied that the two of them were okay, drifted back toward the refreshment table where he had been standing.

"I'm sorry," Marylou said to Bill once they were alone again. "I seem to be more clumsy when I'm with you than I usually am."

"Are you saying I bring out the worst in you?" Bill asked. "It's okay. There is one thing I'll say for you, Marylou Watkins; things are definitely never dull when you're around." He put his arm around her. "Come on, let's dance."

As Marylou danced with Bill, she thought about that moment right before the bales of hay had fallen. She was really sorry that the falling hay had ruined the moment when Bill was about to kiss her. *Just my awful luck,* she thought dryly, *a guy gets ready to kiss*

me and instead gets hit in the head with a
bale of hay!

She still didn't know for sure if it had been
Bill who had driven by her house—but she
almost didn't care. She was having a perfect
time with him.

When the dance ended, they stood side by
side as Mr. Roland got up on stage with the
disc jockey and grabbed a microphone. "Can
I have your attention, please?" Mr. Roland
waited for the crowd to quiet down. "I wanted
to take this opportunity to thank you all for
coming to our dance this evening and supporting our great football team." Mr. Roland
smiled as all the students cheered enthusiastically. "At this time I'd like to give the microphone to our MVP of the night, defensive
tackle Bill Sanders. Come on up here, Bill!"

Bill blushed and made his way up to the
stage, while Marylou clapped her hands along
with the rest of the kids. He took the microphone from Mr. Roland, looking ill at ease,
his blond hair gleaming in the spotlight that
was focused on him.

Marylou smiled brightly, proud that he was
her date, and proud to be with him because
he was handsome and fun, and a really nice
guy.

Bill cleared his throat and smiled shyly at

the crowd of kids. "Uh . . . first of all I'd like to thank all of you for coming to the game and supporting the team. Part of the fun and excitement of being on a football team is knowing there's a big crowd of fans cheering in the stands. I'd also like to thank my fellow team players. Thanks to you, we're number one!" He grinned as the crowd went wild, cheering and clapping enthusiastically. "And last but not least," he continued when everyone had quieted down, "I want to thank a very special girl. . . ."

Marylou felt her heart expand in her chest. *He's talking about me in front of all these people*, she thought in amazement. *He really is my mystery guy, and he's going to tell everyone here tonight that I'm special to him!*

"I want to give a special thanks to head cheerleader, Michelle Osgood." Bill grinned at Michelle, who was standing near the stage.

Marylou's smile froze on her face. *Michelle Osgood? She's the special girl in Bill's life? Then what am I, chopped liver?*

Marylou watched in disbelief as Michelle squealed, ran up onto the stage, and threw her arms around Bill's neck. The kids all yelled and cheered as Michelle kissed Bill on the cheek, then looked directly at Marylou with a smug, triumphant smile.

"Oh, don't they make a cute couple?" Marylou overheard a girl say next to her.

The star tackle of the football team and the head cheerleader make a real cute couple, Marylou thought, a choking sensation welling in her throat. *But where does that leave me?* With a strangled sob, Marylou turned and ran for the privacy of the bathroom.

Chapter Nine

"So then what happened?" Lori asked Marylou on Monday, while the two girls were eating lunch.

"Well, after I realized that Bill wasn't my mystery guy, I was really depressed. I guess Bill knew I wasn't having any fun, so he took me home and that was the end of our date." Marylou sighed and picked at her taco salad.

Lori lay down her fork and looked at Marylou in relief. "So, now that you know Bill isn't the one, that leaves Chris."

"That should make you very happy," Marylou said glumly.

"I was hoping all along that it would be

Chris," Lori agreed, "but you don't sound very happy about it."

Marylou shrugged. "I guess I really liked Bill. I had so much fun with him, and he made me laugh."

Lori speared a tomato with her fork. "So if you like Bill so much, forget about Chris! Go for it!"

Marylou looked at her friend in surprise. "That doesn't sound like you. Besides, I can't forget about Chris, not if he's really the one who drove by my house and gave me the flowers." Marylou sighed. "Lori, I thought about this all day yesterday, since I couldn't get in touch with you to talk about it." Lori had gone to visit her aunt on Sunday, so this was the first real opportunity the girls had had to talk about Marylou's date with Bill. "I really like Bill, but I won't be satisfied until I get a chance to date my secret admirer, who I now know is Chris Mayfield."

"Personally, I think you and Chris would make a perfect couple. He's so organized and together. He'd be a super influence on you!" Lori observed.

"Are you insinuating that I'm not organized and together?" Marylou asked with a grin.

"Well . . ." Lori laughed. "Anyway, I know a perfect way for you to get to know Chris."

"How?" Marylou asked.

"Judy Welch has pneumonia," Lori said with a little smile.

"That's terrible!" Marylou exclaimed, wondering how on earth Judy's having pneumonia could help her with Chris.

"So, Judy has pneumonia, and she also has the lead in the junior class play, which is taking place in six days."

"What does all this have to do with me?" Marylou asked impatiently, poking her salad around with her fork.

"They're having emergency tryouts in the auditorium today after school. If you get the part, that would give you the opportunity to really spend a lot of time with Chris!" Lori grinned at her proudly, as if she had personally arranged the situation for her friend.

Emergency tryouts . . . and Chris Mayfield was the director! Marylou thought about getting the chance to work with Chris. It could be really intense and romantic working with Chris and dating him as well.

"This could be the opportunity you've been waiting for," Lori said softly, as if reading her thoughts.

"You know, I think you're right," Marylou said thoughtfully.

"The only problem is you won't be the only

one trying out for the part," Lori said with a worried frown. "Do you think you can handle the competition?"

Marylou looked at Lori confidently. "I'm sure I'll be a natural!"

"Yeah, a natural disaster just waiting to happen!" Lori replied dryly.

Marylou stood outside the auditorium's double doors, pausing a moment to work up her courage. She had a sudden vision of herself freezing up and not being able to utter a word in front of a huge roomful of people. *This is crazy,* she thought. *I'm not an actress!* But Marylou knew there was no way she could pass this up—it was the perfect chance to get to know Chris. He *was* awfully cute and talented and . . . Marylou smiled. *If he's in love with me, then he might be the guy I've been waiting for. . . .* Marylou took a deep breath, squared her shoulders, swung open the doors to the auditorium, and strode in, trying to appear more confident than she felt.

The auditorium itself was dark, with lights focused on the stage at the front of the room. Scenery and props on the stage formed a living room where four kids were rehearsing a scene.

"Stop! Hold it!" Chris's voice filled the large

room and he jumped up from the first row of seats. Marylou quickly slid into a seat at the back of the auditorium. She watched with interest as Chris ran nimbly up the five stairs at the side and onto the stage. "Laura, I can't hear a word you're saying, and I'm only sitting in the front row. What about the people in the back row? They won't be able to hear a single word. You have to project your voice so that it carries to every corner of the auditorium!"

Laura, a girl Marylou recognized as a senior, nodded her head solemnly.

"And Matt, you have to move further downstage when you say the line 'I won't give up so easily. I love her.'" Chris didn't wait for Matt to answer. Instead he busied himself moving the coffee table an inch to the right and the sofa an inch to the left. He stood back and looked at the adjustments he had made, then nodded. "Okay, let's take it from the top again."

As the four actors began the scene once again, Marylou found she couldn't keep her eyes off Chris, who stood at the side of the stage watching the action. The stage lights reflected off his rich copper-colored hair, and he seemed to radiate energy. There was never a moment when he was perfectly still. He was always tapping his foot, gesturing with his hands, or shouting directions. Marylou had never seen a high school boy with quite so much charisma.

Marylou finally turned her attention to the scene unfolding on the stage. From what she had heard about the play, it was supposed to be some sort of modern-day *Romeo and Juliet.*

The rehearsal lasted about an hour, but the time flew by quickly for Marylou. She was fascinated with the way Chris could find some small detail, even an awkward inflection in an actor's voice, and change it, resulting in a considerably improved scene. *He's really good at this,* she thought in amazement.

Marylou noticed that there were several girls sitting in the first few rows of seats. *They must be here to audition for Judy's role too,* she thought. But the competition really didn't bother her. After all, she wasn't as interested in the part as she was in Chris.

She blinked as the bright auditorium lights suddenly came on. "Okay, gang, that's it for now," Chris said. "Remember, there are only five more rehearsals until the performance!" As the four kids onstage left, Chris turned his attention to the girls sitting in the audience. "I hope you're all here to try out for the role of Miranda. As you've all probably heard, we're sort of in a bind since Judy got sick." When he scanned the group of girls, his eyes seemed to linger on Marylou. He grinned. "Why don't you all move down here and we'll get started with these auditions. Every minute that goes by brings us closer to opening night without a leading lady!"

Marylou moved down to the front of the auditorium with the other six girls. They all sat down in the front row and looked at Chris expectantly.

"I'm going to give you each three pages of the script. I'll give you about ten minutes to look it over, then we'll begin," Chris explained, moving down the line of girls and handing a copy to each of them. "After you've had a chance to look over the lines, I'll send you all outside and call you in to audition individually. Any questions?"

The girls all looked at each other with nervous smiles, but nobody had any questions. Chris nodded in satisfaction, then disappeared behind stage.

"I can't believe I'm here," the girl sitting next to Marylou exclaimed. "I tried out the first time and didn't get a part, so it's probably silly for me to be trying out again."

"You never know—you might be lucky this

time," Marylou said with an encouraging smile.

"Yeah, maybe you're right!" The girl smiled at Marylou gratefully, then went back to work on the script.

Marylou scanned the script, easily memorizing all of Miranda's lines. This was definitely one of those times when having a photographic memory came in handy. It was a gift that Marylou had pretty much always taken for granted. It wasn't until seventh grade that she realized not everyone had the ability to memorize a page of material in just a few minutes, and that her fellow classmates had to spend three times as long as she did studying for tests.

"Time's up, girls." Chris reappeared onstage and the girls moaned and groaned. Several of them begged for a few more minutes to study the scripts.

"Give your names to Scott on your way out, and we'll call you in one at a time," Chris instructed, pointing to a tall boy at the back of the room. "Cathy, you stay here."

"Oh, no, I can't believe I'm first!" the girl named Cathy wailed.

Marylou filed out with the rest of the girls, giving Scott her name as she left the auditorium.

Once they were standing in the corridor, none of the girls talked. Instead they took the opportunity to continue studying the scripts. Marylou scanned hers a few more times, feeling nervous tension tighten her stomach muscles. She really didn't want the part, but it was intoxicating to think about getting to work with Chris for the next six days. After all, she was now almost one hundred percent sure that Chris was her mystery guy. She shivered suddenly, remembering the way his gaze had lingered on her when he had first surveyed the girls who'd shown up for tryouts. It had been a special look, and it had been just for her!

All the girls turned as Scott stepped out of the auditorium. "Sarah Goodman," he said, and another girl went into the auditorium for her audition.

One by one the girls disappeared into the auditorium, then came out, until only Marylou was left. By the time Scott called her name, she had decided the whole idea of auditioning was a big mistake—surely there was another way to get together with Chris.

Marylou followed Scott down the aisle to the stage, then she climbed the steps and walked to where Chris was smiling at her expectantly.

"Let's start. I'll read the part of Jason," Chris said, and Marylou nodded. They had only done about half the scene when Chris stopped her.

"You haven't looked at your script once," he said.

Marylou shrugged nervously. "Do you want me to? Did I make a mistake?"

"No, no mistake," he said hurriedly. "I'd heard . . . but I didn't believe . . ." He shook his head, not finishing what he was about to say. He took Marylou's hand in his and gazed at her. "The role of Miranda is yours," he said, squeezing her hand gently. "Marylou, I'm *so* glad you came."

If that's not proof that he's my special guy, I don't know what is, she thought happily. It felt so great to know for sure—her frustrating experiences with Jesse and Bill had almost been worth it. Now she no longer had to worry about finding her true love—her relationship with Chris was well on its way to being perfect!

Chapter Ten

"Marylou, I can't hear you!" Chris called impatiently from the back of the theater.

Marylou flushed. This was the fourth time they'd run through this particular scene and still Chris wasn't satisfied. She took a deep breath. "My parents must never know that we are still seeing each other," she said to Craig Conner, who was playing the hero.

"I still can't hear you," Chris interrupted again. "Project, Marylou, project!"

Marylou stomped her foot in frustration. "I don't know what possessed me to audition for this play! I'm no actress!"

"Perfect; great projection. I could hear every word." Chris laughed and moved quickly down the aisle toward the stage. "And you auditioned because you knew how desperately I needed you!" He grinned at her, ignoring the whoops and catcalls of the cast and crew. Marylou felt a warm blush cover her face. "We'll break for tonight, gang, but everyone be here right after school tomorrow—and plan on staying late." He turned back to Marylou. "How about if I buy my favorite leading lady a pizza and a soda?"

"Okay," Marylou answered, her spirits rising. Now that was the kind of invitation she'd been waiting for, an opportunity to spend some time alone with Chris. Last night's rehearsal had been strictly business. And today's had been work, work, work!

They both grabbed their coats and together walked out the side exit of the auditorium and into the cold evening air.

"Only three more rehearsals until showtime. Tomorrow, Friday night, and Saturday's dress rehearsal," Chris said as they approached his dark-blue Mustang.

"Don't remind me," Marylou said with a shudder of nervous anxiety. "I'll never be ready in time. I'll probably blow the whole play for everyone!"

Chris grasped her arm and whirled her around to face him, a determined look on his face. "You'll be great. I can't believe you've already memorized all the lines. You're a wonderful girl, Marylou, and you're going to be totally fantastic on Saturday night." He leaned over and gave her forehead a loud, smacking kiss. "Now come on, stop worrying and let's go get that pizza!"

Marylou got into the Mustang on the passenger side and waited for Chris to walk around and get behind the wheel. She gently touched the spot on her forehead where he had kissed her. *He's definitely the one*, she thought.

She smiled brightly at him and fastened her seat belt as he started the car.

"It's a good thing you and Judy are about the same size so the costume committee won't have to go crazy altering all the costumes," Chris said, steering the car in the direction of Alfredo's Italian Restaurant.

"Yeah, that's good," Marylou replied, though she was only half listening to what he was saying. *If only there were a way to be one hundred percent certain that Chris is the one,* she thought. *The flowers!* The idea suddenly popped into her head. If Chris really was her secret admirer, the guy who drove by her house and left her the daisies, then there might very well be some dead daisy petals someplace in the car!

"Remind me to tell Larry, the guy on the lights, to use pink gels for the graveyard scene in act two," Chris mumbled. "Don't you think pink tones will make the scene more touching?"

"Uh . . . yeah," Marylou answered, her eyes scanning the dark-blue interior of the car in search of any evidence.

"I also have to talk to Ralph about getting a vase or something for that coffee table in act one," Chris said. "Maybe we could stick a bunch of daisies or something in it. Would you make a note of that, Marylou?"

Daisies! Marylou thought excitedly. She nodded, her attention focused on a small brown something near her right foot on the carpeting. Was that a flower petal? She lunged forward, grunting slightly as she fought against the restraint of the seat belt.

"What are you doing?" Chris asked, slowing the car down and looking at Marylou.

"Oh . . . uh . . . I think I dropped my earring," Marylou stuttered, grabbing the brown thing off the carpeting. She frowned, realizing it was just a small clump of dried dirt. *Darn!*

"It should be pretty easy to find—I just vacuumed the whole car two days ago," Chris remarked.

Marylou sat up slowly, trying not to show her excitement. Chris had to be the one! His vacuum job obviously would have removed any remaining evidence.

"Did you find it?" Chris asked, pulling into the parking lot at Alfredo's.

"No, I just remembered I didn't put any earrings on this morning," Marylou explained, hoping she didn't sound like a total idiot.

"Well, that's good," he said, eyeing her strangely. Chris turned off the car engine and he and Marylou got out of the car.

On Friday and Saturday nights, the restaurant was always crowded. But as they walked inside, Marylou quickly realized the place was pretty dead on a Wednesday evening. Only a couple of the tables were occupied with kids, quietly studying or talking, and the volume of the jukebox was softer than it was on weekends.

"Come on, let's get a table in the back so we won't be disturbed." Chris guided Marylou to a secluded corner of the restaurant.

This is about as romantic as Alfredo's can get, Marylou thought excitedly as she sat down at the small table. A candle flickered in the center, casting a warm glow on the tabletop.

As Chris sat down in the chair across from her, she tried to hide her smile. The candlelight made his red hair glimmer, and the freckles across his nose seemed more pronounced. *Of course, he's not as good-looking as Bill*, Marylou reflected, then quickly pushed this unkind thought from her mind. She didn't want to think about Bill and the fun she'd had with him at the dance last Saturday night. Bill wasn't her mystery guy, and he didn't love her like Chris did. She and Chris both looked up as a waitress appeared at the side of their table.

"We'll have a medium mushroom pizza and two Cokes," Chris said without hesitation.

Marylou felt a tiny twinge of irritation. *He could have at least asked me what kind of pizza I like*, she thought. *It's a good thing I like mushrooms.* Her irritation quickly disappeared as the waitress left the table and Chris reached across the tabletop and took Marylou's hands in his.

This is it, Marylou suddenly thought, her heart beginning to beat rapidly. *Now he's going to tell me that I'm his dream girl and he's been secretly in love with me for a long time.*

"Marylou . . . there's something I want to tell you," Chris began hesitantly, his thumb drawing small circles on the back of her hand.

"What, Chris?" She smiled at him encouragingly, eager to hear his next words. She bit her bottom lip nervously as she realized the romantic confession she'd been waiting for was now at hand.

"Marylou . . ." he began, looking down at the table as if suddenly shy. He looked back up at her and took a deep breath. "I'm just not pleased with your performance in scene five of act three."

"*What?*" Marylou stared at him in disbelief. She couldn't have been more surprised if he'd told her that her face had turned green.

"Now, don't get upset," Chris said hurriedly. "I know you've only had two rehearsals, but we really have to work on that scene. You've got to relax a little bit more when you're on stage. You look pretty uptight and nervous, and that will come across to the audience."

"Well, I am uptight and nervous on stage," Marylou exclaimed, snatching her hands away from his. Disappointment welled up in her throat.

"Ah, Marylou, don't be mad." Chris looked at her appealingly. "I'm the director. I have to be concerned about your performance. This play is really important to me and I want everything and everyone to be absolutely perfect!" He took her hands again, his eyes somber as he looked at her. "I'm telling you this as your director, but personally, I think you're a terrific girl!"

Marylou felt the hurt dissipating somewhat. It seemed pretty logical to assume that Chris might be shy at declaring his innermost feelings for her. After all, driving by a girl's house and anonymously throwing flowers on her lawn wasn't exactly the mark of an extroverted kind of guy. *He's just shy, and it's natural that his first priority right now is the play,* she thought. She smiled at him warmly and leaned forward in her chair. "Okay, Mr. Director, tell me what to do to make your play worthy of a Tony award."

"So, are you nervous about tomorrow?" Lori asked Marylou at school Friday morning.

"I'm scared to death!" Marylou admitted. "Everyone's going crazy because there's still so much to do before the first performance."

"I called you at nine-thirty last night and your mom said you weren't home yet," Lori said.

"After rehearsal Chris took me out for ice

cream," Marylou explained. "I didn't get home until almost ten-thirty." She stopped at her locker and withdrew a book for her math class.

"Wednesday night, pizza. Thursday night, ice cream. It sounds like your romance with Chris is really heating up," Lori commented, grinning impishly.

"I guess," Marylou said with a sigh as she leaned against a row of lockers. "Actually, I wouldn't call my romance with Chris particularly hot."

"What do you mean?" Lori slammed the locker door and looked at Marylou curiously.

"I don't know, Chris is just so caught up with the play." Marylou frowned in frustration. "It's all he talks about—even when it's just the two of us together."

"I'd say that's quite natural, since he *is* in charge of the play. I'm sure it's very important to him right now," Lori assured Marylou.

"Yeah, I guess," Marylou answered dully. "It's just that when I imagined discovering the identity of the guy who drove by my house that night, I thought things would be more romantic between us."

"Give Chris time. Maybe once the play is over he'll be as romantic as he is in your fantasies," Lori said as the two of them started walking down the hall toward their fifth-period classes.

"Maybe you're right," Marylou agreed. She stopped walking abruptly as she and Lori turned a corner in the hallway.

"What's wrong?" Lori asked.

"I . . . I don't want to walk down this hallway. Let's go around the other way," Marylou said faintly, her gaze on the couple not twenty feet away from her.

Lori followed Marylou's gaze and frowned. "Let me guess—you don't want to walk down this hall because Bill and Michelle are down there together?"

"Brilliant deduction, Sherlock," Marylou hissed, grabbing Lori's arm and yanking her in the opposite direction. There was no way she wanted to walk past Bill and Michelle while they were leaning against a locker gazing deeply into each other's eyes.

"What is with you, Marylou? Chris is your mystery guy; isn't he the one you want to be with?" Lori asked, sounding totally confused as they continued walking.

"Of course he is!" Marylou said passionately. "I just don't feel quite ready to face Bill after last Saturday night." She didn't want to tell Lori that she was afraid Bill would be able to see that she still liked him. "Chris is a fantastic person. Any guy who would drive by my house and throw flowers on the lawn is the guy for me! Come on, let's get to class," Marylou said, relieved as the warning bell rang. "I don't care anything about Bill Sanders. I don't!" she repeated, as Lori gave her a dubious look.

Chapter Eleven

"Wow, you sure look different!" Peggy, who played one of Marylou's best friends in the play, looked at Marylou with a grin.

"I do, don't I?" Marylou said nervously. "I don't look anything like myself."

"With your hair swept over to one side like that and that black sequined evening gown, you look a lot older and more sophisticated," Peggy observed as she quickly did her dark red hair in a French braid.

Marylou nodded and smoothed her hands down the sides of the elegant formal gown. The clothes she was wearing were like no clothes she had ever worn in her life. And even though the waist of the gown had been altered with safety pins and the hem had been basted that very afternoon, she had to admit she looked terrific! *Now, if only I can remember all my stage directions, I'll be fine,* she thought, nervously applying a thick coat of Pan-Cake makeup to her pale face. She realized that most people would be worrying about remembering their lines at this moment. But what concerned her now was remembering Chris's comments so that her performance would please him.

As she worked on her makeup, she ignored all the activity going on around her and out in the hallways. It was amazing to her that the audience already seated in the auditorium couldn't hear the commotion of the crew at work setting up last-minute props on stage.

"I should never have looked," she said nervously, remembering the crowd she had seen in the audience when she had peeked out from behind the heavy velvet curtains moments earlier.

Peggy grinned at her. "I never look out at the audience before a performance. If I see all the people, I feel like I'm going to throw up." She expertly applied purple eyeliner, which Marylou noticed really flattered her green eyes.

"That's how I feel right now," Marylou admitted.

"Flowers for our leading lady." One of the prop girls came into the dressing room carrying a bouquet of daisies. Marylou looked up in surprise.

"Oh, wow! Who are they from?" Peggy exclaimed, giving Marylou an envious look.

Marylou took the bouquet of flowers and searched the leaves for a card. "There's no card," she said, hiding her smile by raising the daisies up to her nose. There was no card, but she knew who they were from!

Peggy looked at Marylou curiously. "A secret admirer, huh? You don't know who sent them to you?" she asked.

Marylou smiled and propped the flowers against the mirror, then went back to applying her stage makeup. "I have a pretty good idea who sent them," she said casually, hoping Peggy wouldn't press her to talk anymore about it. After all, Chris had sent the flowers anonymously, so Marylou didn't feel right about blabbing his name to just anyone.

"Fifteen minutes until curtain," a voice called from the hall, and Peggy quickly turned to the mirror to finish her makeup.

He's such a find, Marylou thought with a smile, her gaze lingering on the bouquet of flowers. *How sweet and thoughtful of Chris to send me a bouquet of daisies right before the performance!* She knew that tonight was going to be a wonderful night. Chris was going to take her to a special party after the performance and they'd have a really fabulous time together.

When she was finished with her makeup, she stepped back from the mirror and admired herself.

"If you'll take a little of that white highlighter and put a tiny drop in the corners of your eyes, it'll make your eyes look larger and livelier onstage," Peggy suggested.

"Thanks," Marylou said, grateful for any task that would keep her mind off the fact that the play would begin in a few minutes.

"Everybody ready?" Chris stuck his head in the door of the dressing room. He grinned at Marylou and stepped inside the room. "Marylou, you look terrific, just like Miranda should look! I can't even tell that the dress is being held together by a bunch of safety pins!" He grabbed her by the hands and whirled her around in a circle, laughing with excitement. "Tonight is going to be the absolute high point of my life, thanks to you!" He released her hands and stepped back. "Just do it like you did this morning in dress rehearsal," he said, running a hand through his coppery hair. Marylou stifled a giggle when she saw that his hair was now sticking up in spikes, making him look like a mischievous little boy.

"Chris, I want to thank you for the—" Marylou began, but was interrupted by a loud voice.

"Two minutes until curtain. Everyone to their places!"

"I've got to go," Chris smiled apologetically. "I've got a million things to check before curtain. We'll talk after the play," he promised, then left abruptly.

Marylou nervously wiped her sweaty palms down the sides of her dress. There would be plenty of time later on to thank Chris for the flowers—and for him to confess his love for her. At the moment, the only thing Marylou had to worry about was getting through the play without tripping over the scenery or falling off the stage!

"For the rest of my life, I will live with the joy of knowing that somebody loved me." Marylou's voice rang out as she lowered her head dramatically. There was a moment of silence, then the audience began cheering and clapping enthusiastically.

I did it! Marylou breathed a sigh of relief, bowing with a radiant smile as the audience shouted their approval for her and the cast members who joined her onstage. *We all did it!* She laughed with excitement and bowed once again, smiling at Craig, who looked as overwhelmed by all the applause as she felt.

As the curtain came down for the final time, all the cast members yelled and cheered exuberantly and congratulated each other.

Their cheering increased as Chris appeared onstage, holding up his hands for silence and grinning at them. When they had all quieted down, Chris looked at them proudly. "You were all fantastic! I can't tell you how proud I am of all of you!" He grinned as they all cheered once again. "And I think we all owe a special round of applause to this little lady right here." He walked over and threw his arm around Marylou's shoulders. "She stepped in for Judy and saved us from having to scrap the whole play." He looked at her, his eyes gleaming brightly. "Marylou, you were magnificent!" He kissed her soundly on the lips and Marylou blushed as everyone hooted and hollered. "Okay, that's it, everyone. Thanks again . . . the play was a huge success!"

As all the kids began to leave the stage, Chris turned to Marylou. "I've got several things to take care of, but I'll come by the dressing room for you in about twenty minutes, okay?"

"Okay," Marylou answered breathlessly, her eyes shining brightly.

Marylou didn't walk back to the dressing rooms—she floated. The whole night had been an experience beyond her wildest dreams. She'd been the star of a play. And now she had a special date with her dream guy, a guy who really loved her! Could life get any better than this?

Once she got back into the dressing room, she had a million things to do to get ready for her special date with Chris. But she wasn't prepared for the crowd of people who made their way into the dressing room to congratulate her.

"Oh, honey, you were terrific!"

Marylou grinned at her parents as they entered the room, their faces beaming with pride.

"I can't believe what a wonderful actress we've raised," her dad said as he grabbed her in a big bear hug.

"Better than the actresses in those dumb horror movies you like to watch?" Marylou teased.

"Definitely!" Mr. Watkins laughed. "It was well worth taking the night off from the store."

"And getting your dad to take a night off is no small feat!" Mrs. Watkins hugged her tightly. "We are so proud of you!" Mrs. Watkins squeezed her daughter close. "Now we're leaving, so you can have a chance to greet all your other fans. I think I saw Lori fighting her way through the crowd to get backstage."

Marylou smiled at her parents. "Thanks for coming and I'm glad you liked the play. I'll be home later, okay?"

Her parents both nodded. "Enjoy the cast party," Mrs. Watkins said with a wink.

The minute they were gone, Lori burst into the room. "I can't believe you pulled it off." She beamed at her friend proudly. "In fact, you were really quite good."

"Thanks, Lori," Marylou said, suddenly anxious as she realized the minutes were ticking by and she still had to change clothes and scrub her face.

"Actually, I thought the whole concept of the play was quite good. Chris obviously put a lot of thought into the script," Lori added.

Marylou gave her an apologetic smile. "Lori, I'd love to stand here and discuss all the complexities of the play with you, but . . ."

"Oh, of course. You've got your little romance on your mind." Lori rolled her eyes and grinned at Marylou. "I hope the night turns out the way you want it to. I really do, Marylou."

"Thanks." Marylou smiled warmly at her friend. "But there's no way the night is going to go like I want it to if I don't get changed and wash this gook off my face before Chris comes by to get me."

"Okay, I'm out of here—off to the computer center to extricate dear Walt." Lori smiled. "Call me tomorrow. I want to hear every detail of your date with Chris!"

"First thing in the morning," Marylou promised.

When Lori was gone, Marylou flew into action, scrubbing her face vigorously at the sink in the corner. "It's no wonder so many movie stars have problems with their skin if they have to wear this thick junk on their face all the time," she said to Peggy, who was standing in front of the mirror and carefully taking off her eye makeup with remover.

"I heard a lot of the movie stars have to go to a doctor for face peels because of their makeup," Peggy said.

"Face peels!" Marylou looked at Peggy in horror.

Peggy giggled at Marylou's expression. "They don't peel off their faces," she explained. "They just take off the dead layer of skin or something like that."

Marylou grimaced. "That sounds totally gross!"

"Everything went really well tonight, didn't it?" Peggy said, switching positions with Marylou. "I love acting," she added, turning on the water.

"Not me," Marylou laughed. "Tonight was terrific, but it's not an experience I want to repeat very soon. Right before it was time for me to go onstage for the first time, I was so scared I really thought I was going to throw up!" Marylou checked the lock on the dressing room door, then changed out of her costume. "I'm not cut out to be an actress!"

Peggy shrugged her shoulders. "It's not the right thing for everybody. Personally, it's the only thing I want to do with my life."

Marylou nodded and grabbed the dress that was hanging on a hanger from an exposed pipe in the ceiling of the dressing room. The dress was new, a surprise from her mother and father. Her mother had brought it home from the boutique on Friday night, saying that the star of a play needed a pretty dress to wear to parties afterward. Marylou smiled as she slipped into the dress. She had to admit, her mom had great taste, and she never failed to choose something that looked exceptionally well on Marylou. This dress was made of a black tweed-like material and had a wide black waistband that cinched her slender waist.

"Wow, nice dress," Peggy commented as she pulled on a pair of jeans and an oversized sweatshirt.

"Thanks. My mom bought it for me," Marylou said, spritzing herself with a purse-size bottle of her favorite perfume, *Eau Jeune.* She smiled at her reflection in the mirror. *Tonight is going to be a special night,* she thought. *I've been waiting all my life for a special guy, and I think I've finally found him. Now that the play is over, hopefully Chris will only have romance and me on his mind.* Her smile widened as her gaze fell on the bouquet of daisies. It was going to be wonderful to be dating somebody as thoughtful and caring as Chris.

She jumped at the sound of a knock on the dressing room door. "You girls decent?" Chris yelled.

Marylou quickly unlocked the door and opened it. Her bright smile faltered slightly as she looked at Chris. He was dressed in the same pair of sloppy jeans and sweatshirt he had worn during the play. Marylou suddenly felt terribly overdressed in her pretty dress and dainty high heels.

"Wow, you look nice," Chris said, stepping into the dressing room.

"Thanks," Marylou answered hesitantly. Had she somehow gotten her signals crossed? He had told her about a special cast party. *Maybe he's going home to change before we go*, she thought.

"Are you ready to go?" he asked, smiling at Marylou.

"Sure," Marylou said, her heart jumping as Chris grabbed her hand.

"Then let's go!" Chris pulled her out of the dressing room and threw an arm around her shoulders. "You were amazing tonight."

Marylou smiled up at him. "That's because I had such a terrific director," she told him, shivering slightly as they stepped out of the school building and into the brisk night air.

"Cold?" Chris grinned and pulled her closer to him.

It was excitement rather than the cold that had made her shiver, but Marylou wasn't about to tell him that. Instead, she enjoyed the feeling of being held close to him. "I'll get the heater started in the car," Chris said, and Marylou nodded happily.

This is going to be the most wonderful night of my life, Marylou thought as she and Chris got into his Mustang. *We'll go to this party and have some fun together, and maybe we'll leave early and spend some time alone.* She shivered again at this thought.

Chris, misinterpreting her shiver, started up the car and turned the heater on full blast. "Ohh, that's cold." Marylou laughed as cold air shot out of the heater vents.

"It'll just take a minute to warm up," Chris laughed.

"Will we be staying long at the party?" Marylou asked shyly, looking forward to spending time alone with Chris afterward.

Chris shrugged. "I don't know, why?" He looked at her in confusion. "Don't you want to go to the party?"

"Oh, sure," Marylou answered hurriedly. She looked out the car window, wondering why they weren't moving. *He must be waiting for the car to get warmed up,* she thought.

She jumped as the back door of the car suddenly flew open. "Okay, I think we're all here," Peggy said as she and a bunch of other kids from the play began to crawl into the backseat of Chris's car.

What's going on? Marylou wondered, looking at Chris in total shock. He didn't look a bit surprised by the fact that his car was being invaded by the entire cast and crew!

"Make room for me." Stan, the two hundred fifty-pound stage manager stood outside the car door.

"There's no more room back here," Peggy giggled.

"Where am I going to ride?" Stan asked worriedly, realizing Peggy was right.

"You can sit up here, Stan," Chris suggested. "You don't mind sitting on Stan's lap, do you, Marylou?" He grinned at her appealingly.

Marylou shook her head numbly, getting out of the car and watching as Stan sat down next to Chris in the bucket seat before he pulled her down on his lap.

"Wow, this is really going to be fun!" somebody cried out from the backseat.

Oh yeah, Marylou thought miserably, shifting positions so that Stan didn't breathe heavily down her back. *This is a real riot.* She wondered how her dream date with Chris had turned so quickly into a nightmare!

Chapter Twelve

"This is a barn," Marylou said in disbelief as Chris pulled the car to a stop and she looked out the window.

"Yeah, isn't it great?" Chris asked enthusiastically. "Peggy's parents said we could have the cast party in their barn."

"They thought that way we could have a lot of fun without worrying about disturbing neighbors," Peggy called from the backseat.

Marylou looked back outside the window, staring at the huge barn silhouetted in the bright moonlight. *I'm going to a party in a barn*, she thought with a sigh. *This is the dream date I've been waiting for with Chris*

. . . just Chris and me . . . and twelve other kids in a barn? She started to close her eyes and lean back, then jerked straight up, remembering that she was sitting on Stan's lap.

"Let's party!" Chris said, getting out of the car, followed by the gang in the backseat. It took Marylou a few minutes to hoist herself up off Stan.

"I'm so psyched!" Chris exclaimed as they all entered the huge barn.

"My parents tried to make it nice for the party," Peggy explained. "They swept the floor, and there's a refreshment table against the wall over there." She gestured to a large folding table against one wall filled with chips and dips, peanuts, brownies, cookies, and other snacks.

A large portable tape player was plugged into a wall outlet. The sound of the local popular rock-and-roll station filled the barn.

"Here comes some more of the gang," Peggy yelled as several more cars pulled up and kids piled out and entered the barn.

Within minutes the party was in full swing. Marylou stood by the snack table, feeling slightly bewildered as she munched her way through a handful of chips and looked around her. *I don't know half the kids at this party,* she thought glumly.

"Are you having a good time?" Peggy joined her at the refreshment table.

"Sure," Marylou said, then added, "I just don't know too many of these kids. Were all of them involved with the play?"

"Yeah, but because you joined the cast so late, you wouldn't know half of them. Some of these kids were on the costume committee, others were in charge of selling the tickets and printing the program."

"Everybody seems to know each other," Marylou said, feeling slightly left out.

"Almost everyone here is a member of the drama club, and most of us have worked together on other plays," Peggy explained.

Marylou nodded, her eyes searching for Chris in the barn full of kids. She finally spotted him, sitting on the floor in a corner, surrounded by several kids who appeared to be listening to him with rapt attention. She could tell by the animation on his face and the lively sparkle in his eyes that he was talking about the theater. He always looked so full of energy when he was talking about his favorite topic.

He hasn't spent one single minute with me since we got here, she thought irritably.

If he's so much in love with me, he sure has a funny way of showing it!

"Is something wrong, Marylou?" Peggy's voice interrupted Marylou's thoughts.

"Oh . . . uh . . . no, I was just thinking to myself," Marylou said, watching as Peggy grabbed a handful of corn chips.

"I love cast parties," Peggy said enthusiastically, popping several corn chips into her mouth and crunching loudly.

Marylou forced herself to smile. "I've never been to a cast party before."

"Cast parties are my favorite kind of parties," Peggy said. "It's great to have fun with kids you've worked so hard with for the past six weeks. It's like all the pressure of the performance is over and everyone can just relax and have a good time."

"It sure looks like our director is enjoying himself," Marylou said, hoping she didn't sound as disappointed as she felt.

"Oh, yeah." Peggy grinned and looked over to where Chris seemed to be demonstrating something to his small audience. He was drawing some sort of diagram in the dirt on the floor. "Chris is really something, isn't he? He wants to direct plays on Broadway someday, and I really think he'll do it. He's so talented and ambitious!"

Marylou looked at Peggy in surprise. "I didn't know Chris wanted to be a Broadway director," she said, wondering why Chris had never told her about his ambition. Wasn't that the sort of thing you told someone you loved? "I guess I really don't know that much about Chris," Marylou confessed, surprised that it was true. They had spent lots of time together in the last week, but they had never really talked about anything personal.

"Tonight's a big night for Chris," Peggy continued. "He's enjoying the limelight and attention that come from being the director of a very successful play."

Marylou nodded thoughtfully. *I'm being a spoiled brat,* she chided herself. *Here I am pouting because Chris hasn't spent any time with me, and tonight is probably the greatest night Chris will have all year! Instead of pouting over here by myself, I should be over there sharing the fun with him.*

She smiled at Peggy and headed toward where Chris was sitting.

"Ah, here she is, the savior of my play." Chris grinned at her and patted the floor next to him, indicating that she should sit down.

Marylou hesitated for only a moment, then sat down on the dirty floor. After all, her dress was already wrinkled from the ride on Stan's lap. At this point a little dirt wouldn't hurt.

As she sat down, Chris grabbed her hand. "Marylou, you were magnificent tonight," he exclaimed, bringing her hand up to his lips and kissing it. Marylou blushed with embarrassment as the kids around them laughed. He stood up suddenly and helped Marylou to her feet. "And now," he announced to the group of kids, "I'm going to dance with my favorite leading lady!"

A slow song was playing on the radio, and Chris pulled Marylou into his arms. He didn't really dance to the music—he just sort of swayed back and forth from one foot to the other. Marylou couldn't help thinking about how well Bill had danced.

"I can't believe how great everything went tonight," Chris said suddenly. Marylou forced herself to pay attention. "I mean, everything just fell together so perfectly."

"I wouldn't exactly say everything just fell together. You worked really hard to make everything turn out the way it did," Marylou said, pulling back from him a little bit and smiling up at him.

"That's true." He smiled back at her. "But a lot of the success of tonight's performance was due to you. If you hadn't been so amazing in learning your lines so quickly, the play would have been a total disaster." He grinned at her. "You even managed not to look uptight and nervous onstage!"

Marylou smiled at him. "The flowers really helped a lot, and I want to thank you for them."

"You're welcome, but what are you talking about?" he asked.

Marylou smiled, thinking he was just teasing. "You know, the daisies that were delivered to the dressing room right before the performance."

Chris shrugged in bewilderment. "That really was a nice thing to do, but I didn't do it."

Marylou stopped dancing and stared at him. "You didn't send me the daisies?"

Chris shook his head.

"Have you ever given me daisies?" Marylou asked, a sick feeling in the pit of her stomach.

"Sorry, you've got the wrong guy," he said with an apologetic smile.

I've got the wrong guy. Marylou stared at Chris, fighting back tears of frustration. She'd been so sure!

"Marylou? What's the matter?" Chris asked.

Marylou just shook her head, too upset to speak for a moment.

Chris gently took her by the arm and led her outside the barn into the quiet of the night. "Now, please tell me what this is all about. Tell me why you're so upset."

Marylou looked up at the bright moon overhead and shivered. She took a few deep breaths to calm herself down. "A couple of weeks ago a blue Mustang just like yours drove by my house and whoever was in it threw a bouquet of daisies on my lawn. I found out that there were three guys who had a car like that—Jesse Wilcox, Bill Sanders, and you." She paused for a moment and wiped away a tear. "I found out that it wasn't Jesse, and it wasn't Bill, and so I figured it had to be you." She thought a moment, then looked at Chris accusingly. "Everything you did and said led me to believe it was you. When I first walked into the auditions for the play, you looked at me and said you were really glad I had come."

Chris flushed and looked at her awkwardly. "That's true. I'd heard that you had an amazing memory, and I knew you were my only hope for replacing Judy. I was thrilled when you showed up for the auditions."

There was a moment of silence. "You must think I'm a total fool." Marylou forced out a little laugh.

"No, I don't," Chris protested, touching her lightly on the shoulder. "I think you're a terrific girl, and if I didn't already have a pretty steady girlfriend, I'd give this admirer of yours a run for his money!"

"Thanks, Chris." Marylou gave him a weak smile, knowing he was trying to make her feel better.

"And you know, I can see how it was easy for you to get the wrong idea about my feelings for you. I have spent a lot of time with you in the last week. You were so nervous about being onstage, I thought you needed extra time and attention. I'm sorry if I led you to believe anything else."

"That's okay," Marylou said with a sigh "One thing I've realized is that you and I could never have a romantic relationship. To tell you the truth, I don't like this theater stuff very much!"

Chris laughed, obviously relieved. "I'll admit, the theater is not for everyone." He paused a minute. "Are you all right?"

Marylou nodded. "Yeah . . . Why don't you go back to the party? I'd like to stay out here alone for a little while."

"Are you sure you're all right?" Chris asked.

"Really, I'm fine." Marylou smiled until Chris nodded and went back into the barn, and then her smile faded and was replaced by a frown of unhappiness.

She looked back up at the moon and wrapped her arms around herself to still another shiver. *Wait until Lori hears about this*, she thought dismally. *I should just give up the search. It was probably only a joke.*

With another deep sigh of frustration, Marylou turned around and went back into the barn to the party.

"I'm sorry you didn't have such a great time tonight," Chris said, breaking the quiet in the car as he drove her home.

"Oh, I had a good time, it just wasn't quite what I'd expected," Marylou answered, biting her bottom lip and staring out the car window.

The very best time I've had for as long as I can remember was with Bill, she thought. *But Bill liked Michelle Osgood*, she reminded herself. There was no hope for her with him. *If I ever find out who this guy is, I think I'll strangle him with my bare hands for all the aggravation he's caused me*, she thought. *But maybe I'll never find out who he is. Maybe I'll live the rest of my life never knowing who it was who gave me flowers and loved me when I was almost sixteen years old.*

"You're terribly quiet," Chris said.

"Sorry, I'm just tired, I guess," Marylou answered.

"Yeah, I'm always exhausted at the end of a play. I think it's because your adrenaline speeds up, and then when it's all over, your body and mind are totally exhausted." Chris smiled at her. "And for what it's worth, I really do think you're a pretty terrific girl."

"Thanks." Marylou smiled back at him. "This girlfriend you mentioned earlier, does she go to our school?"

"No, she goes to Riverfront High," he said, mentioning a high school about twenty miles away.

"Is she interested in theater?" Marylou asked, wanting to keep the conversation flowing so that she wouldn't have to think about how messed up her romantic life was.

"Oh, yeah, she's in all the plays there. She wants to be an actress after she graduates."

"It's nice you two have so much in common," Marylou said, once again struck by how very different she and Chris were. She had been right when she said a relationship between the two of them would never have worked.

"Thanks again, Marylou, for being such a trouper and saving us all in the play," he said as he pulled into her driveway.

"It was a good experience," Marylou said. "At least it taught me that acting is something I don't ever want to do again. It's too nerve-racking!" She opened the car door and got out, then leaned down and smiled at Chris through the open window. "Thank you, Chris, for all your help and support in getting through the play. Someday you're going to be a very famous director and I'll be able to say I knew you when."

Chris smiled with obvious pleasure at her words. "Goodnight, Marylou, and I really hope things work out for you!"

Marylou nodded and stepped away from the car, watching as Chris disappeared into the night. The sight of the fading lights of the Mustang reminded her of the night her mystery man had driven by. *And I know as much about him now as I did that night*, she thought to herself.

She turned and started to walk toward the house, her heart heavy with disappointment. Marylou had just reached her front porch when she heard the unexpected sound of a male voice calling to her from the darkness at the side of her house. She clutched the porch railing, her heart pounding. Who could be lurking around her house at this time of night? The voice called to her again.

"Marylou?"

Chapter Thirteen

"Who is it? Who's there?" She squinted, trying to pierce through the darkness.

"It's me—Bill."

"Bill Sanders, what are you doing hiding out in my yard in the middle of the night?" Marylou asked a little too loudly, stepping down from the front porch and onto the lawn. "You scared me half to death."

"I'm sorry about that, but, Marylou, I have to talk to you. It's really important."

Marylou caught her breath as Bill stepped around the corner of the house and came into her view. He looked so tall and handsome in the moonlight. He was wearing a brown leather jacket and jeans, and was holding a little bouquet of daisies.

"It's you!" Marylou said breathlessly. "I don't believe it."

"Marylou, I don't know what's going on with you and Chris Mayfield, but I can't keep quiet any longer." He stepped closer to Marylou, and in the bright moonlight, she could see the earnest look in his blue eyes. "I know you've been spending a lot of time with him, but I'm not going to just let you go without a fight. So I figured it was time for me to lay my cards on the table."

"Bill, there's nothing going on between Chris and me," Marylou replied, still shocked at her discovery that Bill—handsome, fun Bill—was the guy who had given her the daisies. Still, she was hesitant to let her heart believe it totally. She'd been so sure before—and so wrong! Maybe it was all just a crazy coincidence that Bill showed up here tonight with daisies. "Did you drive by my house a couple of weeks ago and throw a bouquet of flowers on my lawn?" she asked him.

Even in the darkness, she could see the dark blush that covered his face. "Yeah, that was me," he admitted softly.

"And did you have flowers sent backstage

for me tonight?" she pressed, wanting to be one hundred percent certain.

"Yeah, didn't you know they were from me? I signed the card." Bill looked at her curiously.

"There was no card with the flowers," Marylou explained. "I didn't know who had sent them."

Bill slapped his forehead in astonishment. "No wonder you didn't wait for me after the play. I figured when you got the flowers, you'd know how I felt about you. Then when I heard that you had left with Chris, I figured you didn't care." He flushed again, shifting awkwardly from one foot to the other. "You were great in the play tonight."

"Thanks," Marylou replied, pleased that Bill had come to the play. "What did the card with the flowers say?" she asked.

Bill shrugged. "It just said that I wanted to take you out to dinner after the play and that I wanted to talk to you."

"Oh, Bill, I wish I had gotten the card," Marylou said regretfully, thinking of how much she'd have enjoyed going to dinner with Bill.

"The card also told you how I feel about you," Bill added softly.

"And how do you feel about me?" she asked, holding her breath for his answer, and hoping his answer would be the one she wanted to hear.

"I . . . I'm crazy about you. I don't even remember the first time I really noticed you. I knew you were head of the social committee, and I always saw you darting around, working on projects, but we never seemed to be in the same place at the same time!" he said, all in one breath.

"Bill, why didn't you ask me out? Why didn't you just tell me how you felt?" Marylou asked, thinking how much time and trouble he could have saved her.

"I don't know. . . . I guess I was afraid you'd turn me down. It's easy for me to ask out girls I don't really care about, but the thought of asking you out really scared me," Bill confessed. Then he grinned at her. "The best thing that ever happened was when you almost gave me a concussion by falling into me at my locker."

Marylou giggled. "I was afraid I would kill you before I ever got a chance to go out with you."

"All that stuff just made you more special to me," Bill admitted with a small smile, making Marylou's heart expand with happiness.

"I . . . I really like you, Marylou!" he said

145

suddenly, looking awkwardly down at the ground.

Marylou giggled. "I know," she said.

"You know?" Bill looked at her in shock. "What do you mean, you know?"

Marylou sat down on the last step of the front porch, motioning for Bill to join her. "I just happened to be awake and looking out my window the night that a certain blue Mustang drove by my house."

She giggled again as Bill's face reddened. "How embarrassing," he said softly.

"No, it was wonderful, the most wonderful thing that's ever happened to me," Marylou answered.

Bill leaned close to Marylou. "Marylou, I'm totally crazy about you!"

Marylou's heart was beating so loudly in her chest, she was sure he could hear it. Of all the guys she had wanted to be her mystery guy, her first pick had been Bill.

"But what about Michelle?" she asked, suddenly remembering why she had decided that Bill wasn't her secret admirer to begin with.

"Michelle?" Bill looked at her in confusion. "What about Michelle?"

"Well, at the dance that night, you said

that Michelle Osgood was your special girl," Marylou said, a small pout touching her lips.

Bill stared at her in astonishment. "So that's what happened at the dance." He threw back his head and laughed. "Oh, Marylou, it's standard procedure for the MVP of the night to give a special thanks to the head cheerleader. Believe me, that meant nothing!"

"But what about at school? Every time I saw you last week, you were with Michelle." Marylou couldn't forget about that without a full explanation.

Bill grinned at Marylou sheepishly. "I guess I was sort of using Michelle, hoping I'd make you jealous."

"Well, I have a feeling Michelle would like something more," Marylou replied, remembering how smug Michelle had looked when Bill had said she was special.

"It really doesn't matter what Michelle wants," Bill replied. "There's only one girl I want in my life, and she's the girl who ripped my shirt and bruised my nose." He leaned toward her and Marylou knew he was going to kiss her, and she wanted him to kiss her more than anything in the world. As he put his arms around her, she melted against him, not realizing how close to the edge of the step they were standing. Just as his lips were about to touch hers, she lost her balance, and together they tumbled off the step and onto the grass.

"Oh . . . I'm so—" she began, but was interrupted by Bill.

"I know, I know, you're so sorry." He stood up and grinned at her. "And if you think by throwing me off the porch you're going to stop me from kissing you, you've got another think coming!" He helped her up, then pulled her into his arms. "You can break my leg, rip my clothes, and I'm still going to kiss you."

"I was hoping you would say that."

Bill looked around them.

"What are you doing?" Marylou asked, giggling.

Bill grinned down at her. "I'm making sure that there are no cars coming that might run over us, no earthquakes about to take place, nowhere that we can fall, and nothing that can fall on our heads!"

"I think you're safe," Marylou said, suddenly feeling shy.

Bill nodded and slowly his lips moved to hers. Their kiss was everything Marylou had always fantasized about—sweet and tender, and wonderfully exciting.

"You see, I told you that you were safe," she whispered softly as his lips finally left hers.

Bill looked at her tenderly. "Marylou, I don't think I'm ever going to be safe again as long as I'm dating you—and I intend to date you for a very long time to come." He hugged her close against his broad chest.

Marylou snuggled close to him, enjoying the way she seemed to fit so perfectly against him. She had finally found her mystery guy, and the best part was that he turned out to be the guy she had really liked!

"I love you, Marylou," Bill whispered in her ear.

Marylou thought her heart would burst with happiness. *My heart was trying to tell me something all along, and I was just too stupid to listen*, Marylou thought. She smiled up at Bill as his lips claimed hers once again.